For Love
Or Money?

By Sherrie D. Cotton

Copyright © 2009 by Sherrie D. Cotton

Cover Graphic Designed by Gavin Pledger @ www.Gavinpledger.com
757-876-2249

Cover Photo by John Allen III, Atlanta, Georgia

ISBN 978-0-692-00548-4

Published By Sherrie D. Cotton

Write to Author or Order Signed Copy:
P.O Box 83314
Conyers, Georgia 30013

Email us @ newauthor09@yahoo.com

Order your copy online @ www.amazon.com or Barnes and Noble
Website: dramagirlbooks.com
Join Book Club@ dramagirlbooks.ning.com

Printed in the United States of America

Introducing the Author

Author Sherrie D. Cotton grew up in Nashville, Tennessee, in a single parent home. Her father left when she was five. Her mother struggled to raise her and four other siblings alone, but she did it while working full-time. After high school graduation, she couldn't decide what she wanted to do, so she worked a few retail jobs at the Mall. When she turned 21, she moved to Atlanta, Georgia with fifty dollars to her name. She worked at a local drug store to help pay for college along with financial aid. She wasn't "smart" enough to get a scholarship, and she wasn't poor enough to get a "grant". But she *proudly* earned her Associates in Arts Degree/ Fashion Merchandising & Advertising in 1989. In 2003, she decided to go back to school at Kennesaw State University, in Georgia, but she couldn't concentrate because she was going thru a divorce. Being drained mentally and physically, she dropped out. Although she never truly got into the field that she studied, Sherrie still had a passion for it in her heart as well.

After she'd lost her husband thru a devastating divorce in 2004, she began to find herself again. Sherrie volunteered at church in the Missions Ministry, where she was the Assistant in the clothing closet. In 2005, she joined Big Brothers Big Sisters to help someone else less fortunate improve who they are. After a year of successfully being a Big Sister, she decided to help feed the homeless thru the late Reverend "Hosea Williams Feed the Hungry Foundation."

Throughout all the volunteering, and helping others in their time of need, it helped her heal in her own despair. In her leisure time, she couldn't think of what she could do for herself. So, over the years, she read many books by Author's that she admired, and thought, *"I can do that"*. Now today, she is 43 years old, and she has discovered her *new passion* inside of her. She's discovered and developed her skill, gained the knowledge and has the passion for writing. She kept it quiet because there were not many folks around her that would believe in her dream, you know who they are, the *dream killers*.

Thankfully, she has two people beside her that always encouraged her... Morgan, and Shelby, her two precious children. No matter what she went thru, she was very proud to be a single *mom*, and humble *Author!* Additionally, she has created an extraordinary Group called **"NEW AUTHORS ON THE MOVE" and their motto is "EACH ONE TEACH ONE".** *Currently, you can find them on Michael Baisden's website @* ***www.iseecolor.com.***

     In conclusion, do you have overflow? If you have more than one pair of shoes, more than one outfit, a choice of food your blessings are overflowing. Will you share your overflow with someone else? And, remember God instills more than one passion inside of you, which one will manifest in you?

Thank You's

First I'd like to thank God, for giving me life, and instilling in me the gift of writing!

I'd like to thank my daughter Morgan, for always encouraging me!

I'd like to thank my daughter Shelby, who keeps me on my toes!

I'd like to thank my sisters, Terry and Cathy for always being there when I need them!

I'd like to thank my brothers, Michael and William (Billy) who are very caring!

Finally, thank you to my additional family, and wonderful friends, you know who you are!

Hey, Morgan and Shelby mommy did it!

In loving memory of my mother, Nina Jean Storey

FOR LOVE OR MONEY?

Let me introduce myself, I'm Patricia, but my friends call me "Pat". Most of us have "nick-names" that have stuck with us from childhood, given to us from mom, dad, a sibling, relative, friend, a schoolmate, girlfriend or a boyfriend. In my down time I love to sit back, grab a cup of coffee, cappuccino, tea, water, or whatever drinks floats my boat at the time. I'd worked diligently my entire life, and wanted all of what I'd earned. Even though the imminence in my life began to frighten me I thought *"Hmmm, perhaps it was time I got what I really wanted too."*

I'm from a middle-class suburban family who had many struggles trying to stay above water, but we did. I didn't want the same struggles that my family endured, so I chose to go to college to break the curse and pursue my passion for helping woman in the Medical field. I had two sisters; it was five of us in a two-bedroom house. We were a small family for back then. But my Mom and Dad made ends meet collectively. I went to College right out of high school with no breaks in between. I earned my Bachelors Degree at MeHarry Medical College, in Tennessee. I earned my Master's Degree at UCLA. I was accepted into an awesome internship program thru my College career, and eventually earned my Ph. D at Stanford University. I went to undergrad on a Presidential Scholarship. After being tired of campus life, I'd gotten my own little studio apartment, sleeping on an air mattress, very few clothes, and many days eating veggie soup, to keep down cost. My parents were always supportive, but I wanted to do this on my own. Even though my head was always in the books, I'd dated many insufficient guys throughout my college years. They had nothing to offer but their private part, but I didn't have much time for the drama they brought anyway. So, I decided to chill out on dating men for a while, you know, give their broke asses a break.

"Now, I'm going to fast forward my life and go full speed ahead"...so hold on to your seat! You're in for the ride of a lifetime!"

FOR LOVE OR MONEY?

This morning I woke up, a bit tired, but excited about the venture that Michael, my husband and I was finally going on a trip together. It was June, my favorite time of the year where the weather is nice and warm. Michael and I were having marital problems, so we thought we'd take a much-needed vacation together, in hopes of reconciling things, and "getting back to normal", whatever "normal" was. We planned this trip to Hawaii a while back, because we were never at home together. Both of our careers were very demanding, but we knew we needed to vacate our jobs, and spend some quality time with each other. Our marriage was one-of-a-kind, yet along the way, perhaps, somehow our careers got in the way of our "true happiness."

Michael was a hotshot Attorney, who passed the BAR exam with flying colors, and had defended and won hundreds of cases with celebrities over his career. I was a successful and prominent Gynecologist and had won many awards and trophies for "Best Female Obstetrics Gynecologist" of the year! In our own careers, we attended many meetings, conferences, award ceremonies, and events with our Colleagues. We met at a Leadership Conference for Business Professionals in Washington, D.C. We began to date off and on, because either of our careers allotted much leisure time. As time passed, we supported one another when the time allowed. Our family, friends, and peers supported us along the way. I knew that nothing in the world could break us apart, not even our careers! We were successful and inseparable!

Our family consisted of just the two of us. Neither one of us had children; we wanted to be married for a while before starting a family. I was 29, and Michael, my gorgeous husband was 39 years old. I thought our ten-year age difference would be a big issue initially, but it wasn't. Prior to meeting Michael, I'd always enjoyed dating older men; they just seemed to have themselves together financially, emotionally, had their own home, nice car, and great careers! They just seemed to know which way they were going.

Michael was this handsome, self-sufficient, tall thick man, with an award winning chest, biceps, and butt, who stood 6'3" tall, and he weighed 240 pounds. He had a beautiful smile, who carried himself

FOR LOVE OR MONEY?

with great Charisma! He was Christian, very enthusiastic, vivacious, intriguing, and had a huge sensual appeal and a GQ style. He was very well put together, and he knew how to carry himself professional and had the warmest personality. Michael was this private man; who didn't want anyone to know his "personal business". After all he was a hot-shot Lawyer who had come from a wealthy family, with an image to uphold.

Michael wined and dined me often. He brought me elaborate bouquets of flowers, expensive chocolates, warm bubble baths, candle-lit dinners, and uncountable shopping sprees to Rodeo Drive, in Hollywood with limousine service. We went on private jet rides, and numerous luxury trips. He took me to Japan one Valentine's Day, France for my 25th birthday, Mexico for our first Christmas together, and the Caribbean "just because". Michael was so giving that he even bought me a Mercedes as a wedding gift! He said, "I was the apple of his eye," and there wasn't anything that I couldn't have.

Before we got married, one night while I was taking a hot bubble bath, he entered the bathroom, lit candles, put on some soft Jazz, and with his thick juicy lips, he gave me a delicate kiss on my forehead. As he stuck his hand in my bath water and began massaging my feet, washing my feet, massaging my legs, and then he moved up to massage my arms. He dropped rose petals into my bath water, and then he gently took my left hand, and raised my hair off my neck.

"You are so beautiful Patricia." He said looking at her glazed eyes as if she were the only woman on earth!

I smiled from ear to ear, thanking him for the compliment, and then he took my left hand and put it into the bubbly water, rubbing and massaging it. He looked down at me smiling.

"Will you marry me?" Michael asks with confidence.

I paused, and then I raised my hand out of the water where he had slid a 5-carat platinum engagement ring on my finger! I screamed, cried and looked into his eyes.

FOR LOVE OR MONEY?

"Yes, Michael, I will marry you!"

Michael always did it real big. We were both in demanding careers, so he hired a wedding planner so that we would have plenty of quality time with each other. Our wedding was a fairy tale! I felt like Cinderella. No expense was spared. We were wed on a yacht, in Venezuela and I had selected an elaborate white wedding dress trimmed in diamonds, with the back out, a huge train, white satin heels, with a beautiful laced veal. My make-up and hair was flawless. We had a live band that played Jazz and oldies all night, with our most intimate family, friends, and peers that Michael had flown to Venezuela to share in our nuptials. I knew it was every girls dream to wed, but to be wedded like this was indeed a dream!

After we returned from our 14-day honeymoon in Venezuela, we left the airport in Michael's candy apple red Porsche, with a gold tag that read "MB-LAW" (which stood for Michael Brown-Lawyer) but we didn't go directly home. We got into the car in silence and I didn't question where we were going. Slowly, Michael pulled the Porsche over on the side of the road and he reached for my hand.

"Patricia I told you there is nothing that you can't have."

So, he told me to relax and go to sleep, and he blindfolded me, and we drove on this long journey to this secret place. I didn't say a word; I just sat back in the Porsche with the top off and relaxed, with the wind blowing in my hair, trusting the man that I had just married.

Once we arrived (at this secret place), he assisted me in getting out the car. He held my hand, and gently closed the car door. I heard keys jingling, a garage door opening, and I wondered if he was taking me to a warehouse, a new business or what? He had already bought me a new car, so I knew it wasn't that. He finally took off the blindfold from my eyes, and Michael whispered in my ear.

"This is what I had built for you baby!"

FOR LOVE OR MONEY?

And there stood this dream house that I had always wished for as a little girl. There was this extensive glass house, which stood on a hill. A four car garage, surrounded by tall palm trees, a beautiful landscape, plants around the walk-way, with well manicured grass, and our last name already engraved on the mailbox "The Browns". I was so ecstatic that I couldn't wait to see the interior! I knew if the exterior was this fascinating that the interior had to be mind blowing! I reached up to my thick 6'3" handsome husband and gave him the biggest kiss ever!

Michael put the keys in my hand, and we entered the huge two-story home with a basement. The foyer entrance floor was marble, surrounded by lots of tall plants, glass chandelier hanging from a 20-foot ceiling. There was exquisite art decor on the walls, furnished with contemporary leather furniture and huge round tables, that I had seen and admired on a trip we had went to before we got married. A 60 inch flat wide screen TV on the wall with this enormous home entertainment unit and surround sound system throughout the house. Michael had the place decorated for me, and his taste was phenomenal! He not only had the brains of a successful Lawyer, handsome, romantic, sexy, sensitive (to my needs), protective, but hard core on the streets. He had everything that a woman admired and desired.

We walked thru the house holding hands, and each room had its own theme but blending in with the décor of the home! As we walked up the stairs, there was a waterfall on the side of the steps and a see thru pool up above, just off our bedroom. Everything that I could ever dream of was in this house! Michael already had professionals to move my clothes and personal items into the home, so I had nothing to do but go in to see where everything was located.

Our trip back from Venezuela was extremely long, so Michael ran my bath water, and I undressed, got in and just laid back. I told him I loved him, and I would always make sure he was happy.

"Patricia, do you mind if I get into the bath water with you?" said Michael.

FOR LOVE OR MONEY?

"Sure honey, I'd love that." She replied.

He reached into the glass cabinet, pulled out a bottle of white wine, poured us a glass of wine, and he undressed and got into the huge Garden tub, gave me a massage and made passionate love to me.

The days were winding down for our honeymoon to end. We were away for 14 days, and only had a few days left to seek each other's company. Each morning when I woke up Michael had prepared my breakfast.

"Patricia, here's your breakfast baby." And he placed the tray on my lap.

He had gotten up to make me breakfast in bed, which consisted of a flower on the side of my tray, a newspaper, fruit, pancakes, turkey bacon, a poached egg, buttered toast, a napkin folded like a dove, and a short note that read, "I love you Darling." It was evident, that Michael was crazy about me. This man would do anything for me even before I was able to ask.

Michaels' 40th birthday arrived, and I gave him a surprise party. I invited my family and friends, and his family, friends, and co-workers over to our home to help celebrate his big day! He got up early that morning to go into the office to finish up a client's paper work for a big case coming up. It was a Saturday, so I knew he would be gone for a while. I got up early to do my last minute items like wrapping his gifts, decorating the house, and connect with the caterer to be sure they had the address to deliver the food, cake, and beverages. Michael like to social drink, and it was his passion aside of God, his career and me. So, I was sure to order his favorite drinks such as, Wines, Alize, Bacardi, Crown Royal, Beer, white Liquors, and any other beverages I thought he'd and his guest would like.

Once the caterers arrived at 4:00pm, Maria (our house-maid) set everything up. She worked for him before we'd gotten married, but I wasn't too fond of her. I had finished decorating; I just wanted a little bit of my touch in there. The house was clean, because I had Maria to come in two or three times a week for tiding up. We were in a five-bedroom home, with four bathrooms, huge Chef-like kitchen, and formal dining room, steam room, and an outdoor pool. I had no time to do all the manual labor so I told Michael that we needed Maria a few days a week about a month after we were settled in. And, you know how Michael feels about me my wish was his command.

Everything was set up, and Maria, our housemaid did a wonderful job. She was just 25 years old, and an uneducated woman, with no skills. Maria had broken English, did not know how to dress, run over heels on her shoes, and had done domestic work all of her life. Maria was unlike any other uneducated woman, she carried herself with great poise, like she was well educated, pretended to have skills, and spoke very little English to "fit-in". Her figure was very shapely; she had a glowing smile, big beautiful brown eyes, and her long silky curly black hair that fell gracefully around her shoulders. She could have been a model or something more if she had the dream, the means, and enough common sense to go out and get an education. But she seemed quite complacent with just cleaning homes and catering to my every need. After all I was her boss now, and she watched every move that I made, as if she admired me.

As I was getting undressed to bathe, Maria was downstairs in the kitchen area completing her many task for the surprise party tonight, and I ask her to come upstairs.

I hollered, "Maria, I need you to come upstairs for a moment."

I distinctly heard her run over shoes run across the marble floor and she ran up the 20 flights of stairs (as if she had won the lottery) to see what I needed. She entered into my bedroom and saw me naked, and my nipples were protruded, but she quickly covered her eyes. I didn't care if she saw me naked or not, we both had the same anatomy.

"Yes, Madam Patricia, what do you need?" Maria said.

"I need you to run my bath water, get me some clean towels, fresh soap, and lay out me an outfit for tonight's birthday celebration, you know something that Michael will adore."

"Okay, Madam," Maria said.

"Also, I need you to pick out an outfit for Michael too, something to show off his physique."

"Will that be all you require Madam?"

"Yes, for now, now go back and finish the decorating, and be sure all the food is set up properly, and the beverages are at the bar. Oh, and the cake should be here soon, so listen for the doorbell."

"Yes, Madam," said Maria.

Maria was getting tired, and she hated Patricia bossing her around every second. And she wondered how Michael was so sweet to her. He was very giving and caring; she didn't see how he could tolerate such behavior from the woman he loved. But Patricia didn't act aggressive towards him, so he never saw this side of her. Michael was still at the office preparing for a big case. But he was sure to be home later.

I had spent the night in the guest bedroom, Friday the night before, because I knew I'd have to do all the work, and she would get all the credit. He had no idea of his surprise birthday party, because they would always go out of town to celebrate special occasions, such as Birthdays, Valentine's Day, etc. I was always left to do the clean up. I hated seeing him wooed by her. Patricia was so selfish, but Michael loved her regardless of all her faults. He couldn't see any of it, because Michael was so madly in love with her.

As I finished up downstairs, it was approximately 7 o'clock pm; I'd been working all day preparing for Michael's Party. I walked back upstairs to choose her an outfit for tonight. She was sitting in her powder room with just thongs on, applying makeup, lip gloss, and eye lashes. Her silicone breast stood out like they were saluting everyone that watched, and many admired her. Michael had paid for her to have implants years ago, even before they'd gotten married. I overheard her talking to her girlfriend on the phone one-day saying that "yeah, that fool paid for me to have implants, let him spend his money," and she began giggling as if she had made a complete idiot of Michael for someone else's enjoyment. I knew he was just too in love for his own good, especially if he bought her implants before they wed. And she managed to never allow him to see how she rudely behaved towards me when he was away.

It was now 8:00p.m, and time for the party to begin. Guest had begun to arrive. I had chosen a soft apple red v-neck Norma Kamali dress, black Stilettos, and a black Prada handbag, with dangling diamond earrings for Patricia. Her luxurious walk-in closet displayed nothing but a designer wardrobe. It certainly was opposite of Michael's. She had rows and rows of designer clothes, and shoes, several minks, stylish purses and lavish diamonds. He had the smaller walk-in closet with minimal space, which did contain many nice pieces. But Patricia didn't care, as long as she was satisfied first.

As I completed selecting Patricia's party wear, I walked into Michael's small walk-in closet and selected a Hugo Boss black tailored suit, with black and white Stacy Adams shoes, white cuffed shirt, with gold cuff links. He wore a small diamond studded earring in his left ear, and he looked very elegant once he was all put together. When I came out of Michael's Closet, I heard people laughing outside, and then the doorbell ring.

"Maria get that!" Patricia yelled.

"Okay Madam," said Maria.

I thought, *"Okay, anything to get her to shut her mouth"*. And I wisped down the stairs to answer the door. I heard them talking thru the glass door about their husbands. It was Patricia's sisters Renee, and Laura. Renee was married, and had a mean husband, that worked all the time (so he says), so she came without him. Laura had a perfect marriage, a lovely husband, but he was obligated to a prior engagement. Maria opened the huge glass door.

"Ahhhh, Ola, my senoritas!" Maria said.

Renee was hateful like Patricia, and she replied in a nasty tone.

"Ola to you too Maria" now where is Pat?" Renee said.

Laura was easy going, respectful and soft-spoken, unlike Renee.

"Hello, Miss Maria how are you tonight?" Laura said.

"I'm doing well, please come in and have a seat." Maria replied.

And she escorted Laura to the living room sofa. Renee was screaming thru the house. Maria and Laura discreetly rolled their eyes at her.

"Pat, Pat, Pat, where you at girl?" shouted Renee.

Pat shouted down the stairs "hold on girl, I'm coming."

Laura and Maria just looked at each other with disgust, and Maria offered Laura a glass of white wine.

"Would you like some wine Laura?" Maria asks.

"Oh, yes, with these two, I may need the whole bottle tonight!"

Maria giggled, as she poured the wine, handed Laura her glass, and she walked away. Renee was looking out the window at the pool, wanting to take a dip to cool off, but forgot her bathing suit.

Renee said to Maria, "hey, why didn't you offer me something to drink?"

Maria replied, "I'm sorry, Madam, what would you like?"

FOR LOVE OR MONEY?

"Hmmm, uh give me some vodka on the rocks, and hurry up." Renee said.

"Yes Madam, right away."

It was now 10:30p.m and all the guest that were invited had arrived, and was eating, drinking, and dancing. Patricia's best friend Yolanda was standing around just staring at everyone, especially Michael's tall handsome friend, Kenny. Michael still wasn't home. Patricia had been dressed up, waiting patiently, drinking, and eager to sing "Happy Birthday" to Michael all evening long. She wanted him to see what a celebration she had laid out for him. Finally, Michael walks thru the door with much surprise.

"Wow, what's going on here?" Michael said, smiling showing his perfect pearly white teeth.

Patricia was angry, drunk, and disgusted that he had been out all day working. Patricia staggers up to him in her stilettos with a fresh pedicure.

"It's your surprise birthday party; I planned it all by myself just for you." She said.

"Oh, thank you baby." Michael said.

And he gave her a huge hug and kiss in front of their entire guest. It was approximately 75 people at their home who had been waiting for hours for him to come home. Patricia pretended to smile outwardly, knowing that she was pissed off inside.

"Well, you better go get dressed sweetheart, your guest has been waiting for quite some time." Patricia said.

"Okay babe, I'll take a quick shower, and I'll be right down, excuse me."

He turned from Patricia's alcohol breath, and poured him a drink walked up the stairs and Patricia yelled out.

"I already laid out your Hugo Boss suit for you honey." Knowing that was a lie and Maria had done it all.

"Okay thanks babe, I'll be right down." Michael said.

All of their guests were mingling, while Maria was upstairs cleaning up their bathroom, after the mess that Patricia had made prior to getting dressed. Maria was bent over into the garden tub, wiping and scrubbing all the dirt that came off of Patricia. Michael walked into the bedroom from such a long day at the office and jumped right out of his designer jeans, polo shirt, Calvin Klein underwear, and dress shoes. Just when Maria got up from washing out the garden tub, Michael walked into the bathroom singing, and drinking butt naked and Maria just stared at him.

"Oh, I'm sorry Maria; I didn't know you were in here." Michael said surprisingly.

"Oh, um, I'm sorry Michael; please don't tell your wife I saw you naked." Maria said.

"Well, sweetie I won't, don't you worry about a thing, it was an honest mistake."

And Maria walked away, closed the door looking flustered and giggling underneath her breath. Maria thought, *"Oh, boy, he sure does have a nice package"*. And she proceeded downstairs to help serve the guest.

Many of the guests were still drinking, swimming, and dancing having the time of their life at Michael's expense. They had shrimp, caviar, crabs, lobster, and an assortment of salads, veggies, fruits, desserts, and drinks. Michael knew the bill was on him, but he never complained. Maria stood by and watched the sights while lighting his candle. Michael walked down the stairs all dressed to impress, and he did; only he didn't know his biggest impression was on Maria.

Patricia said, "Oh, honey, you look so handsome tonight."

FOR LOVE OR MONEY?

Everyone began singing happy birthday, and Michael blew out his candle on his cake, and made a wish. And then everyone applauded him.

"Now come on, it's time for you to open your gifts." Patricia said.

She grabbed him by the hand forcing him to open her gift first. Michael sighed, and he wondered why Patricia was so aggressive tonight. He thought, perhaps it was because she was drinking. But she never acted this way towards him before, especially in front of guest. He opened the gift that Patricia bought him first, it was wrapped so elegantly and he opened it slowly. He peeped inside the box, and it was a Platinum Rolex watch.

He replied, "Oh, thank you baby, this is what I've always wanted."

The Rolex was a surprise but knowing that he had paid for it was not a surprise. He thought, *"I could add it to my watch collection"*, which was satisfying enough.

"Oh, I'm glad you like it honey." said Patricia.

Michael had begun to open the other gifts; they were all unique gifts from expensive golf clubs to polo sweaters, to front row tickets to the Opera.

"Well, thank you very much everybody", I really appreciate this."

Michael locked eyes with Maria, and she looked away, knowing what a hunk he was underneath all those elegant clothes.

As the night grew later, all of their guests were gone. It was about 3 o'clock A.M, and Patricia was drunk, and she crashed on the soft leather sofa. Her loud mouth sister Renee fell asleep on the guest bed, and Laura had went home. She eagerly wanted to see her husband Randy. Maria had finished cleaning and she went outside to the pool area. She was overlooking the waterfall, out into the moonlight, wishing this were her place.

FOR LOVE OR MONEY?

Michael came outside and said, "Are you alright?"

"Yes, why do you ask?" Maria said.

"Well, you seem a bit uneasy all night." Michael said.

"Oh, no, I'm just tired" Maria said.

Michael walked closer to Maria and she felt her heart pounding as if she was in a race.

"Here sweetie, allow me to massage your shoulders." Michael said.

And before Maria could reject him, his big hands and muscular body was touching her and for the first time she felt like a real woman.

"Close your eyes Maria, and just enjoy the moment."

Maria said, "Oh, no, Michael, you have to stop."

"Why?" he ask.

"It's because your wife is inside and if she knew you were giving me a massage she would fire me and kill you!"

"Whatever do you mean? Patricia is a sweetheart." Michael said.

"Perhaps, she is when you are around, but when you are not home, she talks to me and treats me like trash."

"Why didn't you tell me?"

"Well, uh, because I didn't want to lose my job, or cause friction between the two of you."

"Maria, I haven't been happy with Patricia for a long time. And I know she takes me for granted. I have bought her so many gifts, taken her on trips, bought diamonds, cars, house, and put my clients off so

14

that I can give her quality time. But, for some reason it seems like it's just never enough."

Maria turns around, standing 5'3" tall, looking into Michael's eyes.

"Oh, Michael if you were mine, I'd never misuse you."

Michael gently pulled Maria to his chest, and held her in his arms for a moment, and then he pulled her chin up with his finger to give her a gentle kiss on her lips.

Renee woke up to use the restroom and she went to the kitchen for a drink of water, and saw Michael and Maria kissing each other outside on the patio near the pool. Renee snatched the glass door open, and ran outside.

"How dare you cheat on my sister with this low-life maid!" screamed Renee.

"Renee shut up and take your lonesome, drunken ass home," replied Michael.

Maria pleaded with Renee to please not tell Patricia what she saw. She bent to the ground, in humiliation to her knees towards Renee.

"Oh no, I don't want to lose my job Madam."

"Only on one condition." said Renee.

Michael was pissed off, and he intervened, lightly touching Maria's arm to lift her up from the ground.

"What condition?" Michael said.

"If you give me $100,000 dollars, I won't say a word, you'll save your marriage, and Maria will still have her job tomorrow."

FOR LOVE OR MONEY?

Michael shook his head, and agreed. He didn't want to lose everything he had worked so hard for, and he didn't want Maria to lose her job. Plus he loved Patricia, but he was beginning to question his marriage. He thought *"was Patricia in it for love or money?"*

"I have something that you will do for me later too missy," said Renee.

"Okay," replied Maria, stuttering…"anything, anything for you Madam."

Renee got dressed, and was sober enough to drive home at 5:00am. Maria apologized to Michael for the mess she had caused all because she was feeling blue. Patricia had worked her so hard before the party, and she took all the credit for the work that Maria had done.

The next day Patricia got up to go meet a girlfriend at her house in the city. Maria was still asleep. Michael was in the kitchen cooking breakfast as usual, and he heard Patricia stirring her keys around.

"Hey baby, where you going so early?" Ask Michael.

"I gotta go baby" "I'm meeting Yolanda for brunch, and do a little shopping." Patricia said.

"Well, won't you have some breakfast with me first?" Michael asks.

"Oh, no brunch with Yolanda will be plenty," said Patricia.

And she kissed him on the cheek goodbye, leaving a lipstick print on his cheek, turned around quickly and sashayed out the door.

Maria was still downstairs asleep. Michael didn't want the breakfast he'd made for his wife to go to waste, so he thought he'd offer it to Maria. Maria heard a gentle knock at her bedroom door, and it was Michael. She opened the door, and was in shock.

"Oh, Michael, can I help you?" Maria said.

16

FOR LOVE OR MONEY?

"Yes, you can have breakfast with me." Michael said.

"What? Your wife will kill you!" Maria whispered.

"And besides, haven't I gotten you into enough trouble?" Where is Mrs. Patricia anyway?" Maria asks nervously, peeking past Michael thru the door.

"Just relax Maria", and let me do for you for once." Michael said.

Maria looked at him and smiled, and jumped back into bed, as Michael handed her the breakfast tray with a newspaper, a rose, and a letter that said *"I love you"*, which was for Patricia, but she wasn't appreciative of them anymore, so he gave it to Maria.

"Oh, Michael, I think you forgot to take this off."

And she handed him the letter that said, *"I love you"*, which was for Patricia. He'd given her one each time he prepared her breakfast in the morning, along with the newspaper and rose.

Michael said, "You can keep that until you feel the same way about me."

"What! Are you sure you feel this way about me?"

"Well, what about Patricia?" Maria said.

"Yes, I do, and I have for a while. I guess the time was never right for me to express it. Patricia doesn't show affection towards me anymore, and we haven't made love in over six months. Michael said.

Maria sat her breakfast tray to the side, and got up and hugged and kissed him as if he were the only man on earth …her man! She never said it back, but she knew he was a gentleman, and that he would wait for her answer. Maria wanted to be sure of this; after all, Michael was married.

17

FOR LOVE OR MONEY?

The sun was glistering hot! It was 98 degrees, but Patricia and her friend Yolanda were painting the town. After brunch, they hit every store at the Mall using Michael's American Express card.

Yolanda said, "Girl I'm getting tired, it's 6:00, we have to save some of this energy for tonight."

"What's happening tonight?" Patricia said.
"Oh, you didn't know? We are going out tonight. You can wear one of the outfits you just bought, and get dressed at my house. Just call Michael, and tell him where you are, and you know he'll be cool with it."

"Okay." Patricia said. She loved to party, so all she needed to hear was the word *"party"*, and it was on.

The phone rang, and Michael answered.

"Hello Michael?"

"Yes, Patricia, where are you honey?"

"I'm still with Yolanda, and we are going out tonight."

"Well, haven't you been with her all day? When will I get some quality time with you Pat?"

"Oh, you will babe," Yolanda was feeling a bit down, and I told her I'd stay and cheer her up."

"Well, what time should I expect you home?" Michael said.

"…Around midnight okay, good-bye honey."

And she hung up quickly. So, Michael just sat and wondered what the hell was going on with his wife. But he knew the way things were going between them, he'd soon find out.

FOR LOVE OR MONEY?

Maria and Michael had joined each other in breakfast, but she had cleaned their home, and ran out to do errands for the Brown Family. There Michael was sitting, and waiting again for Patricia to come home. He read a book, and then later he ran out to rent a movie.

Patricia and Yolanda were dressed to the nine's! They had on mini-skirts, stilettos, and designer beaded halter-tops, drinking and being treated first class in VIP at Club Strike. After they danced for a while, they sat down to drink. Men were always buying them drinks, and asking them both to dance. Yolanda was the brain behind all of this. She loved to lead; but she wasn't a successful leader in her own life, it was a disaster. Her husband left her years ago for being so wild, and whorish. He finally got fed up with all the partying and he took their three year old and moved. She lost custody of their son, and never tried to get him back. But apparently she didn't care, because she still carried on the same way.

"Come on Pat." said Yolanda.

Patricia said, in a slurred drunken voice "Where are we going?"

"In here." said Yolanda.

So, Yolanda grabbed Patricia by the waist and escorted her into the VIP room upstairs, and she began kissing on her neck, rubbing her back, and lifting her skirt. Patricia was too drunk to stop her, all of a sudden, there was a bright camera flash; someone had taken their picture while they were in their sexual act.

Patricia said, "What the hell was that for?"

"Oh, girl don't mind these fools, just kiss me." Yolanda said. And Patricia did. She was always into women, but never revealed it to Michael.

It was 12 mid-night, and Michael was pacing the floor worried about his wife. She wasn't home, and she didn't answer her cell phone. He looked all over the house to see if Maria was around too, but she wasn't. So, he finally put on his pajama pants and called it a night, still hoping in his heart that she would call or come home soon. He began looking thru her things, in hopes of finding some clue as to what his wife was up to. He called around a few other friends to see if they had heard from her, but nothing. So he finally laid down in their huge king size bed alone tossing and turning, but he finally fell asleep. Michael had always thought if he'd been a good husband, provider, and lover that his wife would always be happy.

It was getting late, and the sun was beginning to rise. Yolanda and Patricia had partied all night. So, Yolanda drove them home. Patricia had slept at Yolanda's place, because it was too late to go home and she was drunk.

It was 6am, and Michael heard keys rattling at the door. He jumped up, put on his robe and went downstairs thinking it was Patricia.

"Oh, Good Morning Michael," said Maria.

"Hey, I thought you were Patricia."

"Why would you think that Michael is she not asleep?"

"No, unfortunately, she didn't come home last night."

Well, have you called her to see if everything is okay?"

"Yes, but she won't answer the damn phone." said Michael.

"Oh, well, I hope everything is alright" Maria Said.

"Well, thanks, me too." said Michael.

"Maria?"

"Yes, Michael."

FOR LOVE OR MONEY?

"Would you have breakfast with me again?"

"Yes, I'd love to," Maria said.

So, Michael began making coffee, and cooking breakfast again. Maria went downstairs to her room to relax a little. She had been out with some friends and wanted to rest a bit. After Michael finished cooking breakfast they sat on the sofa and watched TV, and talked a little bit. About 9a.m. Patricia walked thru the door and Michael jumped up off the sofa. Maria got up and grabbed her blanket, and headed back downstairs as Patricia walked thru the door.

"Hey where the hell have you been all night?" said Michael.

"I stayed all night with Yolanda because I had too much to drink to drive home, I hope you didn't mind?"

"Mind! Mind! Are you out of your damn mind Patricia?" Michael yelled.

"I sat up damn near all night waiting on you, calling, and worried if something could have happened to you." Michael said.

"I'm sorry honey, my battery on my cell phone died, and I didn't have the charger with me."

"Well, you could have used Yolanda's phone you know?"

"I suppose, but I didn't so there." said Patricia.

"Michael, I want to get some rest, I don't want to argue."

"Okay, Patricia, that's fine, go get your rest then."

Michael stormed out of the living room, and went to put on his clothes and he left pissed off and in a hurry.

"Where are you going?" asks Patricia.

"OUT!" yelled Michael "I'm sure you won't mind!" And he slammed the door.

Maria looked out the window as Michael sped off in his Porsche, wishing she could have gone with him, but instead he was alone, as usual. And she was stuck at their house to clean up. Maria knew Michael had been thru so much, his sister-in-law extorted $100,000 from him to keep quiet about the kiss she had seen the night of his birthday celebration, and his wife was now out doing God knows what. So, Maria put on her coat, ran out of their house to follow him. Her car wouldn't go as fast as a Porsche, but she caught up to him in her little Volkswagen. He wasn't going very fast, but she was concerned about his well-being.

Michael looked into his rear view mirror, and pulled over. He saw Maria following him. He got out, and she pulled in right behind him and rolled down her window. He got out of his Porsche, and walked up to her car.

"Maria what are you doing following me?"

"I was just concerned if you were okay or not."

"I'll be okay; would you like to come with me?" said Michael.

"Yes, I'd like that" Maria said.

"Well, follow me," said Michael.

"Okay."

Maria followed Michael a few miles out to a beach Condo off the Santa Monica shore. She had no idea where they were headed, but she knew she wanted to go with fine ass Michael. Once they arrived, Maria looked around and she asks several questions.

"Whose place is this Michael?" asks Maria.

"It's mine. Patricia never knew about it. I always come here to think alone, especially when she's getting on my nerves. Come on, come in." said Michael."

"Okay, you lead the way," said Maria.

Maria walked in and her eyes were in awe of what she saw.

"Wow, this is really nice Michael."

"Oh, thanks, come here," said Michael.

"Oh, no, no," said Maria.

"But I want to hold you."

So, Maria gave in, and allowed Michael to hold her close to his warm thick muscular body, and she felt their hearts beat as one.

"Will you kiss me Maria?"

"What about Patricia?" ask Maria.

"She doesn't love me anymore; she just married me because of what I can give her. Now kiss me." Michael said.

And she did, with her eyes closed so tight that she'd hoped she would never have to open them again. After he kissed her, he took her hands, and showed her around the Condo.

"Oh, this is absolutely beautiful," said Maria.

"Thanks, but not as beautiful as you." said Michael.

Maria blushed, and put her head down. Michael gently lifted her head up with his hand, and told her to never look down when someone compliments you. He taught her how to have self-pride, have confidence in herself, and over time he took her on shopping sprees, out to dinner. But that day they laughed and talked all evening long.

"Well, it's getting late, I guess I better go." said Maria.

"Go, Go where?" Michael said.

"I better let you get some rest."

"Well, I'd rather rest with you here" Michael said.

He began undressing her slowly, picked her up, and took her into the bathroom. He ran her bath water, and lathered her body with bath oil. He washed her up, and dried her off. He helped her get out of the marble bathtub, as he wrapped her body in a huge soft cotton towel.

"Oh, Michael, I feel so relaxed and comfortable with you."

"Shhhh, just relax" said Michael.

Michael oiled her body down, and brushed her hair gently, and he picked her up and placed her on his silk sheets, as she melted into his arms all night long.

Patricia finally woke up after sleeping off her drunkenness all day, but Michael still wasn't home. She was used to him catering to her every need. She knew she messed up, and didn't know how to fix it. Only this time she thought it was too late. She knew she pushed Michael into someone else's arms, because he was beginning to cater to her less and less, but she had no idea who it was.

Patricia was yelling thru the house, "Maria, are you here?"

The house was silent as the night was long, because neither of them was there to cater to Patricia. Both of them were sick of her bossiness. And he was tired of her doing whatever she wanted to do, and all he could do was pay the tab. Patricia called Michael's cell phone, and he answered.

"Hello," answered Michael.

"Hey, it's me, what time are you coming home?" Patricia said.

"I'll be home tomorrow," said Michael.

"Oh, so you still mad at me?"

"Why don't you come home so we can talk?" ask Patricia.

"I'll be home in the morning."

"Okay, I love you Michael." Patricia said, and he hung up the phone.

Just after Patricia called Michael, Yolanda called Patricia to see if she was okay. The phone rang.

"Hello, hey girl, what's happening?" said Yolanda in a loud voice.

"Hey, I'm gonna get you, Michael is mad at me. He stormed outta here, and he is not coming home."

"Well, that's his problem, he'll get over it!" said Yolanda.

Yolanda was always jealous and envious of Patricia's marriage to Michael anyway. All the success they both possessed, the undivided attention he gave her, things he gave her, places they had gone together over the past 6 years. She couldn't have been anything but jealous. Yolanda couldn't keep a man because she liked to party too much, and she was very promiscuous. So, she tried to make sure anyone else that she hung with was as miserable as she was.

"What do you mean he'll get over it? That's my husband you're talking about!" said Patricia.

FOR LOVE OR MONEY?

"Well, if you loved him that much you wouldn't have been with me!"

Patricia was appalled at what she heard come from Yolanda's mouth.

"That's why your dumb ass is alone." Patricia said.

"Oh yeah, and soon you will be too." Yolanda said furious, and she hung up in Patricia's face.

"That bitch!" yelled Patricia.

Her best friend was no longer her friend, and her husband was angry with her at the same time. And she didn't know what to do. The next day Patricia woke up alone, because Michael never came home. She went to work with Michael on her mind, and was thinking about what Yolanda had said to her yesterday.

It was Monday, and Michael was pooped from the long week-end of chasing after Patricia. He had a long workday ahead, but when he got up he realized he was alone in the Condo. Maria had gone home, but he enjoyed her company, and he was alone for once, it was time for reflection, he thought. He knew he wanted a divorce, but he wanted to wait a while to see if Patricia would come around, he truly loved her. But he had begun to have feelings for Maria too. He got up, and jumped into the hot shower. And as he stood there thinking, letting the hot water stream down his muscular body lathered with soap. He washed up, rinsed off and then he got out, dried off and began getting dressed, grabbed his keys and left.

As he was walking out the Condo, his cell phone rang, "Hello" said Michael.

"Hey, who is this?" Michael said.

"It's me, Renee, you got my money nigga?

"Look, let me get you your damn money so you can quit calling me. Meet me at Jackson Park in a half hour."

26

FOR LOVE OR MONEY?

"Okay, be there you bastard," said Renee.

Renee drove so fast to Jackson Park that she got pulled over by the Police for speeding. But since she didn't have a driver's license on her, she was taken to jail. Michael arrived at the Park, and he waited and waited for her, but soon he left. He thought she was full of games. He had gone to the bank to withdraw $100,000 and had a cashier's check so that he could pay off his greedy little sister-in-law that extorted money from him so that she wouldn't tell his wife that she saw him kissing the maid the night of his birthday party. It was his word against hers, but he knew Patricia would believe her own sister over him. Therefore, he just wanted to pay her off for a peace of mind.

Michael wanted so much to have a perfect marriage, and thought he did until recently. Patricia had been distant and inconsiderate hanging in the streets with Yolanda all times of the night.

"Well, I guess she isn't coming, she's full of games." Michael thought. So, he left.

He put the cashiers' check in his brief case in the trunk of his car, and went to work. He had no idea that scandalous Renee was on her way, but was pulled over for speeding with no driver's license and taken to jail for a couple of days.

It was noontime, and Maria called Michael. She was always excited to speak with him. Nobody made Maria's day like Michael did, and he knew it.

"Hello," answered Michael.

"Hi Michael, how are you?"

"Oh, hi Maria, I'm doing well now that I hear your lovely voice." Michael said.

"What are you doing for lunch today?" asks Michael.

"Nothing, what would you like to do?" said Maria.

"Well, meet me at my Condo at 2 o'clock."

"Okay" said Maria. And she pressed "end call" button on her cell phone.

Michael left the office and went home to prepare lunch for Maria. He made some baked almond chicken, fresh shrimp, a Hawaiian salad, and fresh fruit with white wine. He placed it in a huge picnic basket on a blanket on the floor in the living room, with candles lit, and a bouquet of yellow roses spread all over the blanket, which meant friendship. Michael was so romantic that his romance drove whomever he was involved with crazy! They couldn't resist him. He knew just what to say and just what to do! Maria was now getting the royal treatment that she so desired all of her life! Patricia had driven Michael right into her arms. Although it was unplanned, Maria wasn't about to back down now. They had been seeing each other now for a few weeks. And Maria was getting hooked!

Michael heard a knock at the door, and he looked out, and smiled. It was Maria all dressed up, she even had on high heels. She had on the black sultry satin dress he'd bought her and a sweet smelling fragrance when he took her on a shopping spree. He had never seen her so beautiful. As soon as he opened the door, he gently took her in his muscular arms, and held her close, and he gave her a soft kiss on her lips.

"Mhhhh, you smell nice, come in, come this way." Michael said.

He led her by the hand, and took her to the in-doors picnic area he planned at the spur of the moment. Michael was very romantic, and spontaneous. He loved to surprise his woman with things that would make her smile, things that would make her day just a little bit easier.

"Oh, wow!" said Maria.

"Here, take your shoes off, sit down, and relax."

FOR LOVE OR MONEY?

Michael poured Maria a glass of white wine, as they sip together looking in each other's eyes.

"This is so nice Michael," said Maria.

"Well, I'm glad you like it," said Michael.

He proceeded to fix her plate, and unexpectedly, she reached over and kissed him.

"Muah!" Right on his thick juicy lips!

"Well, what was that for?" Michael said.

"It was for you, for always thinking of Me." said Maria.

"Oh, no problem, it's my pleasure to serve you Maria, you deserve it baby."

She grinned from ear to ear thru the entire meal and conversation; trying to be sure she was a lady, and not talking with her mouth full, and keeping her legs close together.

Maria had never been treated so royal, and had so much attention. She was nervous and eating slowly, just so that she could save the moment. This type of romance didn't happen to Maria; after all she was only the maid. She knew she didn't measure up to "Dr. Patricia", but she was better mannered and caring. An hour or so went by, and Michael noticed the time.

"Well, this was delicious, but we have to go. I have to get back to the office. I must meet a client at 5 o'clock."

Maria thought he would want to sleep with her after their romantic lunch, but he didn't he respected her and their friendship. Michael helped her off the blanket, gently placed her shoes back on, blew out the candles, and gave her a sweet hug goodbye.

29

"Thank you for having lunch with me at such short notice" Michael said.

"Oh, its okay, anytime, I enjoyed it." said Maria.

Maria left the Condo smiling for the rest of the day. She ran to her car like a little girl, and called her girlfriend to tell her she had a wonderful lunch date with this handsome hunk of a man, but she couldn't say with whom. She didn't want the word to get out that she had a thing for this married man, her Boss! Besides if word got back to Patricia it would be World War III over her man!

Back at the Medical Office Patricia had a full day at work. She was stressed out from not seeing Michael all week long. It was Friday again, but she managed to get thru each day without him tending to her every need. She had one more client who came in for a pap smear.

"Dr. Patricia Brown?"

"Yes?"

"Your last patient is here to see you." said Sarah, Dr. Brown's Assistant.

"Okay, thank you Sarah would you please send her in and get her prepped for her examination."

"Yes, Ma'am," said Sara.

Dr. Brown's Assistant, Sarah, got the patient prepped for her procedure, and left the room to tend to another patient. Patricia entered the room in a hurry.

"Oh, hi Janice, you're looking lovely today."

"Oh, why thank you Dr. Brown."

"So, how are you?" said Dr. Brown.

FOR LOVE OR MONEY?

"Oh, I'm doing well," said Janice.

"Good, now lay back and open your legs, and let's get started."

Janice put her feet in the stirrups, and before Sarah could get back into the office to observe, Patricia gave Janice a breast exam massaging her breast slowly, and in a sexual manner. And she told Janice to close her eyes, and she moved her hands downward, as she inserted her fingers into Janice's vagina without a surgical glove on.

"What in the world do you think you're doing Dr. Brown?"

"Shhh, its okay honey, lay back and let me finish your exam."

"No thanks, take your filthy hands off of me, I'm getting the hell outta here, and you'll hear from my Lawyer!"

Janice jumped off the table and grabbed her clothes and went flying thru the door with her dress on backwards, and one shoe on. She ran into Sarah in the hallway, and knocked all the papers out of her hand.

"Ms. Janice, where are you going, what's' wrong?" asks Sarah.

But Janice was too upset to tell Sarah what had happened. Sarah went into the exam room, and questioned Dr. Brown about Janice.

"Dr. Brown, what's wrong with Ms. Janice?"

"Oh, she was upset because I told her she had a sexually transmitted disease."

"Oh, bummer, that's why she ran thru the hallway crying hysterically, what a shame." said Sarah.

"I guess her husband gave it to her." said Dr. Brown.

"Yeah, I suppose." said Sarah looking puzzled.

31

FOR LOVE OR MONEY?

"Well you can go home now Sarah. I have to do some paperwork, see you Monday."

"Ok, well, have a good weekend Dr. Brown," said Sarah.

"You too." said Dr. Brown.

Sarah got her things and walked into the lobby, and she saw Janice sitting in a chair by the window with tears streaming down her face.

"Hey, Janice, are you okay, what happened in Dr. Brown's office?

"That lesbian bitch sexually assaulted me!"

"What, what did you say?" said Sarah stuttering.

"She massaged my breast and stuck her fingers in my vagina without gloves on."

"Are you sure? That's some pretty heavy accusations Janice! And Dr. Brown is a great Doctor ya know?"

"Hell yeah, I'm sure, I'm not delusional." said Janice.

"Well, how will you prove it?" asks Sarah.

"I have to talk with my Lawyer, and see what he advises."

"Please let me know what you decide to do, because between you and me, unfortunately, I know a few more patients with the same allegations from the past."

"Oh, really, why didn't they say anything?"

"Because most people are intimidated by Doctor's, especially Dr. Brown, and they have a hard time proving it. But if you want to talk with the other victims, I'll be happy to call them, and hook ya'll up." said Sarah touching Janice's shoulder for comfort.

FOR LOVE OR MONEY?

"Okay," said Janice sniffling and wiping her eyes with her hands.

"Wheeew, oh thank you so much for your help," said Janice with a long deep sigh.

"You're welcome, now calm down, and go wipe off your face and put your dress on correct. I'll wait here for you."

"Okay, thanks Sarah," said Janice.

Janice came out of the bathroom, and she gave Sarah her telephone number and address so that she can call her later with the information on the other victims.

"She will never do this to another patient" said Janice.

Sarah walked Janice to her car, and they both said, "We'll talk later". And got into their cars and drove away.

As soon as Michael finished his 5 o'clock appointment, he got a phone call. He thought it was Renee again about that money, but it was another client. It was Janice. Janice had no idea that Dr. Brown was Michael's wife.

The phone rang, "Hello," answered Michael, with a deep voice.

"Hi Michael, this is Janice."

"Oh, hey Janice, how are you?"

"I'm not so good; I need to set up an appointment with you. I have a problem, something happened today and I need your professional legal advice."

"Okay, no problem, but can it wait? I'm available Monday at 1 o'clock, is that a good time for you?"

"Yes, it is" Janice said.

"Okay, Janice meet me at my office Monday at 1 o'clock." And he gave her directions.

"Okay, I will, see you then."

"Alright, Good-bye" said Michael.

Michael stayed busy; he was one of the best Lawyers on the West Coast. And he had many referrals from clients who he had won many complex cases for over the years. Knowledge was power in his case, because he knew the Law in and out, and to him it was second nature. He was very gregarious, loved helping people, and he got crazy paid for it too!

Patricia was still at the office finishing up her last minute paperwork, hoping that Michael would call her, but he didn't. She had begun to make her life so convoluted that she didn't know whom to turn to. When Patricia got off from work, she called her friend Yolanda. Yolanda was bad news, but Patricia was too ignorant to realize it. Yolanda really had it out for Patricia after the argument they had about Michael and her marriage to him. But Patricia called her because she was lonesome.

Her phone rang. "Hello" answered Yolanda in a nasty tone.

"Hey Yolanda it's me."

"Me who?" said Yolanda.

"It's Pat damit."

What do you want?" said Yolanda.

"I need to talk to you," said Patricia.

"When?" ask Yolanda.

"Now!" yelled Patricia.

34

"Okay, talk," said Yolanda.

"Well, I'd like to see you and talk in person, are you at home?" Ask Patricia.

"Yes."

Yolanda was short with Patricia, she was still pissed off at her from the argument they had. And if Yolanda was mad about something she wanted the whole world to be mad and feel her pain too.

"Well, I'm on my way over there."

"Okay, you better hurry up, I don't have all night." And Yolanda abruptly hung up.

Yolanda controlled Patricia, and Patricia controlled Michael and Maria, at least she did in the past. Now her world was starting to fall apart. Patricia drove fast, but with caution to get to Yolanda's place. She was eager to talk to someone about what was going on. Approximately 40 minutes later Patricia arrived at Yolanda's apartment. She parked, and got out of her Mercedes, walked up the stairs and knocked on the door.

Yolanda yelled, "Who is it?"

"It's Pat, open the damn door."

Patricia was tired of Yolanda's sarcasm. Yolanda looked out and snatched opened the door.

"Hey, I need to talk to you," said Patricia.

"Okay, about what, you and Michael? So, what's wrong this time?" said Yolanda.

Patricia took a seat on the sofa, and looked up at Yolanda with worry in her eyes.

FOR LOVE OR MONEY?

"Girl you won't believe what happened today at work?"

"What?"

"I had a fine ass patient that came in for a pap smear today, and I'd been attracted to her for a while, but never said anything. She really turned me on, and my assistant wasn't in the office, so I began to examine her without gloves on, and she felt so good."

"What are you crazy?!!! Are you trying to get sued and lose your damn license to practice?" "Did she notice it?" said Yolanda.

"Well, yeah, she did notice it, and she got up and ran out of my office, and she said I'll hear from her Lawyer. So, now I don't know what to do."

"Umm, you dumb ass, it's your word against hers right?"

"Well, yeah" said Patricia.

"Soooo, she would have to prove it right?" asks Yolanda.

"But I've done this before to several other women. I'm addicted to women Yolanda. I've never told anyone that before."

Yolanda had a blank look on her face like she just saw a Martian in space!

"If anyone ever finds out I'm doomed. My career will be completely over!" said Patricia.
"Okay, calm down, don't go jumping to conclusions. How would anyone find out?"

"I don't know. If word got out, I'd be sued for every penny I've ever worked for! I'd lose my Medical License and my husband!" Patricia said.

"Well, at this point, the only thing you can do is wait."

"Here let me fix you a drink, a strong drink to take your mind off of this mess."

"Well, now I have to admit, I'm a little jealous," said Yolanda.

"Why is that Yo?"

"Because I thought I was the first and only woman you had ever been with?"

"No, I have been intimate with other women Yolanda, but it's usually when I'm out drunk as hell."

"But, it's weird, because when I'm at work I try not to think about it, but all day I'm looking at these fine ass women. I just can't control myself sometimes. But this time I may have crossed the line."

"Thank God Michael doesn't know I'm bisexual. If he did, he would have been long gone. You know he's Christian and totally against that type of lifestyle. He and I haven't seen each other all week long, and he won't talk to me or even come home. I have no idea where he has been staying." said Patricia.

"It sounds like you have a lot on your plate" said Yolanda, pretending to be sympathetic.

"Yeah, I do."
"Well, come here, and make up with me," said Yolanda rubbing her on the back of the neck.

They both began kissing and rubbing all over each other; they undressed each other and took a shower together. When they stepped out of the shower one by one, Yolanda dried off Patricia, and they made love on Yolanda's sofa for hours.

Michael called Renee to see what happened to her, and she didn't answer her phone. He had no idea she was taken to Jail. But got out a few days later and thinking of what mischievous thing she could do next. He thought she was full of shit as usual. All she wanted was money, she had no interest in if he really loved her sister or not. Once he got home, he rested a while after a hard day at work, and then he called Maria.

"Hello" answered Maria.

"Hey baby, it's me," said Michael.

"Hi Michael, how are you sweetie?"

"I'm fine, I miss you baby."

"I miss you too, I was hoping you'd call." said Maria.

"Oh, most definitely. I wouldn't let the day go by without talking to you love," said Michael.

Maria was eagerly waiting for Michael to ask her over and she wanted to make love to him, but he hasn't made that move. Michael was a perfect gentleman, after all he was still married, but Maria was ready for him, and she couldn't wait to see how he worked it. She had already seen him nude the day of his 40th birthday, but she wondered what he felt like inside her. He had seen her nude too, given her baths, massages, and watched her try on clothes, but they never made love to each other.

"So, what's up with you tonight?" Michael said.

"Oh, I was supposed to hang out with my girlfriend, but she cancelled on me," said Maria.

"Oh, well, I think I'm going to call it a night myself, I'm tired" said Michael.

"I guess you had a long day at the office huh?"

FOR LOVE OR MONEY?

"Yeah it was" said Michael.

"Would you like to go out tomorrow?" ask Michael.

"Yeah, I'd like that, but I have to go to your house and clean up its Saturday remember?" "Madam Patricia would have a fit if I didn't show up. God forbid if she had to lift a finger!"

Maria laughed and she heard Michael snicker because he knew she was telling the truth.

"Why don't you quit?" Michael said.

"Because I won't have an income if I quit."

"Well, you won't have to do that much longer, trust me."

They talked a few more minutes, and Michael was getting sleepy, yet still attentive to Maria. He was moaning and whining for her attention too.

"Babe, I think I better get some rest, good night sweet heart, let's try to meet tomorrow okay?"

"Okay", said Maria.

Maria woke up early Saturday morning with Michael heavy on her mind. She walked into Patricia and Michael's elegant glass house at 6 o'clock A.M, and it was as quiet as a mouse. It seemed weird not to smell breakfast cooking. Michael would always get up early religiously every Saturday morning to cook for Patricia. But the house was empty.

"Hello Madam Patricia, are you here?" said Maria.

No one answered. So, Maria looked in every room to see if Patricia was in another room, but she wasn't. *"Hmmm, I guess Madam stayed out again last night"* Maria thought. And she began to clean

39

each room one by one wishing it were her house with Michael. Once she finished cleaning, she sighed from exhaustion, locked up, called Michael, and left in her beat up Volkswagen.

Patricia woke up around 9 o'clock A.M, and Yolanda woke up beside her with no clothes on. They had been intimate all night.

"Good Morning Yolanda."

"Hey," said Yolanda. She still had a nasty attitude.

"Do you want some coffee?" ask Patricia, like she was the woman, and Yolanda was the man.

Patricia somehow had her priorities all wrong. She was catering to a woman (instead of her own husband) who wished nothing good for her. They were intimate because they were drunk, and Yolanda took in everything Patricia told her the night before very private things that was going on, that could someday be used against her. But Patricia had to confide in someone, should it have been Yolanda? Why not her sister Laura, or Renee? Would she be sorry she ever told?

"I guess I better go home", said Patricia.

"Okay, I'll walk you to the door," said Yolanda hurriedly.

Patricia got dressed, and reached out to give Yolanda a hug good bye, but Yolanda refused the gesture and just closed the door after Patricia walked thru it. So, Patricia slowly walked to her Mercedes, feeling foolish and used again. She got in, and drove home with nothing but Michael on her mind and thinking how she could patch things up.

Patricia felt terrible for what was happening in her life, and she hated how Yolanda treated her, especially after she confided in her last night. She got home and it was sparkling clean. So, she knew Maria had been there. It was about 10 o'clock A.M, and she wondered where Michael was. She called him; the phone rang and he answered her call.

FOR LOVE OR MONEY?

"Hey, I think we need to talk," said Patricia.

"About what?" Michael asks.

"Us," said Patricia.

"Oh, so now you want to talk?"

"Yes, I think we should," said Patricia.

"Okay, I'll be there in an hour," said Michael.

Patricia was excited that her loving husband finally agreed to come home to her. She was hoping to reconcile with Michael, they haven't been together in quite a while. Patricia had been sleeping with her best friend Yolanda, and Maria had wooed Michael. So, there was this huge gap like the Grand Canyon between the two of them.

Patricia went upstairs to freshen up. She showered, and got in the bed like she'd spent the night at home. Michael knew she wasn't at home because he had talked to Maria, and she told him that nobody was home Saturday morning. Patricia put on her pink silk nightgown with pink fuzzy house slippers, and sat up in the bed after she showered. She heard Michael's Porsche pull up in the garage, and her heart began to pound like it was their first date. She peeked out the window and it was him finally.

Michael grabs his overnight bag and entered the house looking around, noticing what a great job Maria had done. He walked up the stairs, and entered the bedroom.

"Hi Honey, I'm glad you finally came home! Here let me take your bag," said Patricia.

Michael ignored the petty talk. "So, what's been going on with you Michael?" Patricia asks.

FOR LOVE OR MONEY?

"Well, you tell me, you're the one who's been MIA, not me."

"Oh, you mean when Yolanda and I go out shopping and dancing?"

"Come on Patricia, don't patronize me, you know damn well what's going on."

"I'm not patronizing you Michael. We have been distant for the past few weeks, and I don't want us to be apart anymore." said Patricia.

"Well, it's a little bit too late for that don't cha think?" Michael said angrily.

"So, what are you saying Michael?"

"You haven't been supportive towards me in a long time Patricia, and you staying out all night just really aggravate me. I would have never done you that way, and you know it. You have been irresponsible, and disrespectful to me. And I'm not putting up with it anymore!"

Michael was stuffing more clothes in his overnight bag, while he was yelling at Patricia.

"What are you doing?" Ask Patricia upset.

"I'm not staying here with you; I need to sort some things out."

As if Michael had not said a thing, Patricia ran her fingers slowly thru her hair trying to seduce her husband and she asks him a question.

"Aren't you going to tell me how pretty I look, and that you miss me and love me?"

"Patricia for the past six years it's been about you and what you want. Well, now it's my turn."

"Now, what does that mean?" said Patricia.

FOR LOVE OR MONEY?

"Oh, you'll see," you'll see!" said Michael.

Michael vigorously walked out of the bedroom after he'd packed more clothes in his bag. He walked down the steps, grabbed his keys off the kitchen counter top and stormed out the door. Patricia ran to the garage door and yelled at him to the top of her lungs.

"You bastard, you haven't heard the last of this!"

"I'm sure I haven't Patricia now go back in the house and put some clothes on, or better yet, go call Yolanda." And he got in his Porsche and drove away.

Patricia stormed back into the house, pissed off that she didn't turn on Michael anymore. She had no idea where he was going, and whom he was staying with, but she knew it wouldn't be home. Michael drove as fast as he could to get back to the Condo to call Maria. Ring, ring, ring, but Maria didn't answer her phone this time. Another call was coming thru to Michael, and he answered it.

"Hello" said Michael.

"Hey, Michael, it's Kenny, down at Club Strike."

"What's up man? I haven't talked to you in a while."

"Yeah, I know, I've been busy managing the club, but I've seen your lovely wife here a lot with Yolanda."

"Oh, yeah?" said Michael.

"Yeah, but I have something I think you might want to see" said Kenny.

"Okay, well, I'm not too far away, I'll come right over."

"Okay, I'll be here," said Kenny.

FOR LOVE OR MONEY?

Michael was on his way to his Condo, but he made a u-turn in the middle of the street to head back to Kenny's nightclub. After driving a few extra miles, Michael drove up, and parked immediately in the first space. He jumped out of his Porsche, hit the remote alarm switch and ran into the club, but nobody was in sight.

"Hello, is anybody here?" shouted Michael.

Kenny walked down the stairs, looking good with an envelope in his hand, not wasting any time.

"Hey Bro what's up?" said Kenny.

"Not much man, what's up? What you got that you want me to see?"

"I know this is going to hurt, but I couldn't let it continue without telling you man" said Kenny.

And Kenny handed Michael the thick brown envelope. Michael opened the envelope, and to his surprise he saw pictures of Patricia and Yolanda groping all over each other, kissing, and hugging. One photo showed Yolanda's hand underneath Patricia's dress with her panties near her knees.

"What the hell is this?" Yelled Michael, what's going on Kenny?" said Michael.

"Well, the word around here is that Patricia has been sleeping with her best friend Yolanda. And you knew Yolanda was a lesbian right?" said Kenny.

Michael was astonished. "Hell no, I didn't!"

"I thought her and my wife were just good friends all these years!"
"How long has this shit been going on behind my back, and why didn't you tell me?" said Michael?

FOR LOVE OR MONEY?

"Calm down! Well, I knew I had to come to you correct, with evidence, so I had to get evidence first."

Michael got really quiet, breathing hard and he was raving mad.

"Are you alright man?" ask Kenny.

"Yeah, I'm just really shocked and disappointed in Patricia. I can't believe this shit! My own wife cheating on me, and not with a man, but with a woman, her best damn friend! I'm not sure which is worse!"

Michael was furious at Patricia. "How could she do this to me with all I've done for her? I've done nothing but love her!"

Michael began to shed a tear, but he caught it before it hit his crispy white Ralph Lauren shirt. He was devastated. And even though he had been dining with Maria, he never slept with her. Michael had class, and he was definitely a gentleman, and Maria enjoyed every minute of him.

"Okay, well, I appreciate you for telling me this shit man. At least somebody was looking out for me."

"Oh, no problem man, I hope you get it straightened out," said Kenny.

Michael walked out of the club with his head down, feeling as low as anybody could. He knew he still loved his wife, but he was falling in love with Maria. He got on his cell phone and called Maria again, and she finally answered.

"Hello" answered Maria.

"Hey baby, where you at?" Michael said.

"Oh, I'm on my way home." said Maria. But she could hear in his voice that something was wrong.

"What's wrong sweetheart?"

FOR LOVE OR MONEY?

"I need you to come to my Condo as soon as you can."

"I will I'm on my way."

Maria dropped everything she was doing to go see Michael. They were really starting to fall in love and they hated seeing each other hurt. Anytime he needed her she was there.

"Okay, I'll see you in a while." said Michael, and they hung up.

Michael was driving slow, holding up traffic. Cars were blowing at him, and going around him. He didn't care; he had just heard the worse news of his life that his wife was cheating on him with another woman! Michael finally made it home, unsure of how he made it, because he didn't even remember driving. He was still shocked by the news he had just heard from Kenny. He got out the car slowly, grabbed his bag, and walked in and dropped his bag on the floor. And he lay on the sofa with his arm propped across his head, with his eyes closed. He had fallen asleep, and his doorbell rang. He jumped up off the sofa and looked out, it was Maria. He opened the door to let her in.

"Hi babe" said Michael.

"Hey, you look awful, what's wrong?" said Maria, as she closed the door behind her.

"You will not believe what I just found out?"

"What, you're scaring me? Maria said.

"Here look at these", and he handed her the brown envelope.

Maria opened the envelope, not sure what to expect. She pulled the contents out, and saw pictures. She looked at them and asks who the people were in the photos.

"Who is this Michael?"

FOR LOVE OR MONEY?

"Look at them Maria, look at them closely."

"Well, this looks like Patricia, but she's engaged with another woman," said Maria.

"Yeah, and look at the other woman" said Michael.

"Oh, my God that's Yolanda, her best friend!"

"Oh, my goodness Michael, I'm so sorry! How did you get these?" said Maria.

"A friend gave them to me."

Michael knew not to call out names. He didn't want Kenny's name involved in any of this mess. So, he just replied *"a friend"*.

"Well, what are you going to do?" Ask Maria.

"I am going to divorce her, on grounds of infidelity. I have my proof right here, and she won't get a dime from me!"

Maria just held Michael close in her arms, and she didn't say a word. She just listened to him vent all evening, and they fell asleep on the sofa together.

It was getting late, and Maria had to go. She didn't want to spend the night unless Michael asks her to. He needed some space to think things thru. They woke up all snuggled together, and sweaty.

"I'm going home tonight, call me tomorrow okay?"

"Okay, you know I will." said Michael. And he walked her out, and watched her drive away.

Sunday morning Michael had intended on going to church, but he overslept. He was so beat-down from the news he had found out yesterday about Patricia. He laid around watching TV all day, and then he got up to shower, grabbed a bite to eat, and got prepared for Monday. He phoned Maria, as promised, and they spoke briefly, because he had a meeting with a prospective client Janice at 1:00 the next day and he wanted to be sure he was prepared and prompt.

Monday morning arrived, and he got up and fixed himself a continental breakfast. He called Maria after a hot cup of coffee and a plain bagel.

"Hey Maria, how are you this morning?"

"Fine, now that I hear your voice." said Maria.

"Are you okay?" Maria asks.

"Yes, I am. I have an appointment today, so hopefully we can meet after I finish up at the office."

"That sounds great!" said Maria.

"Okay, see you later then," said Michael.

"Good bye, try to have a peaceful day," said Maria.

"Okay, I will, you too," said Michael, and they hung up.

Janice was at the office waiting for Michael an hour early. She was so nervous and wanted so desperately to get help. She just couldn't believe what had happened to her at Dr. Brown's office last week. Michael arrived at the office at 12 noon, and he saw Janice sitting in the lobby waiting.

"Hi Janice, you're here a bit early."

"Hi Michael, yeah I couldn't rest all weekend, I really need to talk to you."

"Okay, well, come on in," said Michael standing tall, looking down at her.
Janice grabbed her things, and got up and followed Michael into his office, and she sat in the reception hall.

"Give me a minute to settle in, and I'll be right with you."

"Yes, sir" said Janice.

Michael stirred around his office; open the window blinds, turned on his desk lamp, made some clean space on his desk and pulled up a chair to his desk.

"I'm ready won't you come in" said Michael.

"Yes, thank you," said Janice.

"Please have a seat," and he pointed to the chair.

"So, how can I assist you?"

"Well, this is very bizarre what I'm about to tell you, so please bear with me."

"Okay" Michael replied.

"Well, Friday I had an appointment with my OBGYN Doctor. And as I was waiting for the Assistant to come back into the examining room to observe, the Dr. rushed in first. She closed the door, and proceeded to examine me. She placed her hands on both of my breast and she began massaging my breast in a sexual manner."

Janice was having a panic attack and she began to breathe hard.

"It's okay, slow down, I'm listening." Michael said. And Janice took a deep breath.

"Okay, well all of a sudden, she closed her eyes, and she moved her hand down my stomach, and stuck her fingers in my private area without gloves on, as if she were climaxing by touching me," explained Janice.

"Are you sure that's what you encountered?" ask Michael.

"Yes, sir, I can tell if a glove is on or not, and she rubbed my breast, instead of examining them. The touch was totally different than what I had ever experienced in my life!"

"Well, Ms. Janice, let's document all of this for our record, to build our case, and we will contact your Doctor by letter regarding this matter."

"Okay," nodding her head in agreement.

Michael was great at Law, and he knew exactly how to build his case. Although he was tired himself, he didn't allow his personal life to interfere with his business.

"Okay, so begin by telling me the date, time, reason for your visit, what procedure you had done, Dr's name, how long you have been seeing this particular Dr, the location of the office, etc."

Janice began to speak, but she cleared her throat several times, because she was nervous that nobody would believe her, not even her Attorney. But she answered each question that Michael asks her.

"Okay, it was approximately 5 o'clock P.M, Friday evening on August 7th. I was the last patient of the day. It was time for my annual pap smear, and I was to be checked to be sure everything was normal. I'd been a patient for a little over a year and never had a problem before. I'd gotten undressed (as usual) and sat on the examining table, spread my legs, and put them in the stirrups. But before the PA could come in the office to observe the procedure, the Doctor came in, closed the door and started groping me."

"Is it standard procedure for the PA to be in the exam room while the Dr. is examining you?"

"Yes." said Janice.

"Okay, what area of town is this office in?" said Michael.

"It's North of here." replied Janice.

"That's a nice side of town, very Prominent Physicians in that area." Michael said.

Michael was surprised this kind of thing would happen in that area of town.

"What's the address there?"

"It's 2241 Briar Mill Lake, San Diego, California," replied Janice.

"Oh 2241, I'm familiar with that area and office, what's the Doctor's name?"

Janice paused, and sighed, and she said "Dr. Patricia Brown." After documenting the last comment, he dropped his ink pen on the desk.

"Excuse me" Michael said.

"It's Dr. Patricia Brown."

"Oh My God! You've got to be kidding?" said Michael.

"I knew you wouldn't believe me," said Janice.

"No, it's not that I don't believe you, it's just that Dr. Patricia Brown is my wife!"

"Oh, no" thought Janice. "I'm sorry Michael, I had no idea."

"It's okay, I'm sorry too," Michael said sympathetically.

"Unfortunately, we've been having marital issues anyway, and I'm soon asking her for a divorce."

"I hope I didn't stir up more trouble for you. Should I see another Lawyer?"

"No you don't have to, unless it makes you uncomfortable?" said Michael.

"I'm okay with it, as long as you are?" said Janice.

"Yes, I'll take your case Janice, you definitely have one."

"I just found out that she is bisexual and has been sleeping with one of her girlfriends for quite sometime."

"I'm so sorry to hear that Michael. I had no idea Dr. Brown was your wife either. And I sure had no idea that she liked women!"

"Well, join the club, I didn't either" said Michael.

"I shouldn't be telling you this but; a friend of mine gave me photos of her engaging in sexual behavior with another woman."

"Wow that must have really hurt?" said Janice.

"Yes, it did."

"So, where do we go from here?" Ask Janice.

Still maintaining his professionalism, Michael said, "Well, let me document a few more things, and I will start your case. My office will contact Dr. Brown with documents served by the Deputy. But to get started, I will need a $2,000.00 retainer fee and you to sign this contract."

FOR LOVE OR MONEY?

"Okay", said Janice. And she began writing out a check.

"Is this going to be difficult for you to defend me against your wife?"
"Wrong is wrong, and business is business" said Michael.

"You just make sure you hold it together, and not talk to anyone about what's going on or we could possibly lose our case."

"Mums the word," said Janice. And she handed Michael the check for her retainer fee, and she sympathized for him, and thanked Michael for his time.

"I'll be contacting you soon Janice, and I'm sorry this happened to you" said Michael.

"Okay, thank you, and try to have a good day yourself" said Janice.

"Thanks" Michael replied.

Michael reached out to shake Janice's hand. As their hands touched, they both knew they were betrayed together. As Janice walked out of Michael's office, he put his face in his hands in a disarray state of mind. He just could not believe his own wife (whom he cared for and loved so deeply) would do such a thing! She had sabotaged their marriage for the last time.

Michael sat back in his chair after Janice left his office and thought *"Whew! I can't believe that low down dirty cheating bisexual wife of mine. After all I've done for her, now this. And that dyke Yolanda, she was never my friend; she wanted my wife all along. I'll show them, I'll show them both not to mess with me".* Michael finished up his last minute paper work on Janice L. Wood's case, closed the office and went home.

It had been a long day, and Michael just wanted to rest from all the drama he'd heard about his wife over the past few days. He was in shock that his own wife was cheating and bisexual. He arrived at his Condo, and cleaned up before calling Maria. He knew his work was cut out for him with this new case he had just taken for Janice. Plus he had to deal with filing for a divorce. So, he went into his office at home, and began the paper work for his divorce. It took all night, and he never had time to call Maria.

As usual he made sure all his ducks were in a row. He knew Patricia wouldn't agree to a divorce, especially for infidelity without a fight. So he was preparing for what all he knew that was in store for him in Court. He had a written statement and documented the allegations from Janice. The photo's he had of her with Yolanda, and Kenny was going to testify against her in court. Other women had come forth with the same allegations about Dr. Brown regarding things they had faced in her office over the years, so things were looking favorable for Michael. He had money, stocks and bonds in a Brazilian account that she didn't know about, the Condo on the coast, a boat, and two local savings accounts with millions of dollars in each of them, with only his name on it. He made damn sure that she wouldn't see a dime of it.

It was Thursday morning and Patricia didn't have any early morning patients, so she slept in late. She got up, pranced around the house, wondering if and when Michael would call her. She fixed her a cup of cappuccino, slipped on her designer robe and went to the mailbox. She pulled out this white envelope wondering, *"What is this? It's addressed to me, from Michael's office. Hmmm, I wonder what this could be."* As she walked back to the house, she began opening the envelope. *"Ouch"* cried Patricia. She was in such a hurry to see what it was that she slit her finger opening the envelope. It was a letter showing Janice L. Woods –VS- Dr. Patricia Brown. She went into the house, and began reading the letter, and thought, *"Oh, that skinny little bitch filed a sexual harassment case against me! But I wonder how she knows Michael!!!"* All she cared about was how she knew her husband; she wasn't concerned that she could ruin her reputation and lose her practice.

After reading the sexual harassment letter, she went to grab a band-aid for her finger, but there was a knock at the door. She thought *"damn who could this be so early?"* and she answered it.

54

"Yes, who is it?" Patricia replied yelling thru the door.

"It's the San-Diego Deputy; I need you to open the door." She proceeded to open the door.

"Yes, how can I help you sir?" ask Patricia.

"Hi Ma'am, are you Dr. Patricia Brown?"

"Yes, I am, why?"

"I have a summons for you to appear in Court, you need to sign for it."

The Deputy pointed to the document and handed her an ink pen, "You need to sign here," and she did.

"Thank you, have a good day ma'am," said the Deputy, and he walked down the long driveway, got back into his squad car, and drove away.

Patricia went into the house, closed the door, and plopped down on the leather sofa. She opened the thick vanilla envelope and it had additional documents in it of complaints against her, showing who, what happened, where, time, dates, etc. So, needless to say she felt angry and scared. She whispered to herself, *"Oh, my God, there are twenty-two sexual harassment complaints against me, what am I going to do?"* So, she got on the phone in a hurry and called her Lawyer.

The week had flown by, and Michael had worked his behind off. New clients and new cases, plus his own drama his wife was putting him thru took a toll on him, but he kept going strong. He had completed the divorce papers, and went to file them at the courthouse downtown. Patricia had been calling him all week trying to find out how he knew Janice. But he ignored her calls. Michael had the Divorce papers served to Patricia on her job to be sure she got them. The receptionist was sitting at the desk, listening to Rapp music, painting her acrylic nails when the Deputy walked in.

FOR LOVE OR MONEY?

"Hello, Welcome to Dr. Brown's Office, how may I help you?"

"Yes, I need to see Dr. Patricia Brown please."

The Receptionist replied "Okay could you have a seat, I'll get her for you?" "May I ask what this is regarding?"

"Yes, the San Diego Police Department has some forms that require her signature."

"Oh, okay, hold on please," said the receptionist.

She got up to go back to get Dr. Brown, hoping to not mess up her freshly painted nails, wrinkle her pleather skirt or miss her favorite Rapp song.

"Dr. Brown, the San Diego Deputy is here to see you."

"Oh, Okay, thanks Regina, I'll be right out."

Regina walked back out to her desk, plopped down at the reception desk, blowing her nails dry, and she looked into the lobby at the Deputy.

"She'll be right out." said Regina.

Dr. Brown peeked around the corner, and then she entered the waiting area, rubbing her sweaty palms down her white medical coat.

"Hello, I'm Dr. Brown, how may I assist you?"

"Yes, Ma'am, we have a letter for you, and we need your signature here." pointing at the paper for her signature.

"What is this for, May I ask?"

"It's from Attorney Michael Brown's Office."

FOR LOVE OR MONEY?

'Oh, okay."

Patricia nervously signed the form, and said "thanks."

As the Deputy nodded his head, he turned away and walked out of the office. Patricia went back to her office, opened the letter and it was documents from Michael serving her for a divorce on grounds of infidelity. *"Oh, he will never be able to prove this!"* she thought. *I'll take him for everything he has. I'll get the house, the Porsche, and alimony. He will always continue to take care of what he started.*

Dr. Brown put away the letter, and walked to the receptionist area and whispered to Regina.

"Regina, could you cancel the remainder of my appointments for today and reschedule them for another day?" Regina had an attitude. She thought Dr. Brown was going to tell her to turn the music down.

"Oh, yes, Ma'am, right away" said Regina surprisingly.

Sarah and Regina knew something was wrong, because of all the drama and gossip that was spread throughout the office. The Deputy showing up, she was starting to cancel appointments, show up late for work, or not come in at all. Patients were complaining and stopped coming into her office. Her practice was beginning to dwindle. There were mostly old women coming in now. Dr. Brown had come on to so many of her young patients that they were afraid to continue seeing her. Patricia wasn't attracted to the old ones, so they had no idea what was happening. It was business as usual for them.

Patricia said "Goodnight" to her staff, and grabbed her Gucci purse, and Dune & Burke carrying case, packed everything she knew she would need, rushed out of the office, and got into her Mercedes. She immediately called Michael even before she started her engine.

"Hello" said Michael. He was in the middle of lunch with a client.

"Hey you dirty bastard, I got your divorce notice today."

He paused and said "I'll have to call you back; I'm in the middle of lunch with a client."

Patricia yelled "I don't give a shit, I need to talk to you now!" in her harsh demanding voice.

"Like I said, I'll call you back," and he hung up in her face.

Michael was having lunch with Kenny explaining to him what was going on.

'Wow, she's upset huh?"

"Yeah she is" said Michael.

"Well, like I said I will testify against her in court bro if that's what you need me to do." said Kenny.

"Okay man, I appreciate you." Michael said.

"Oh, no problem man, that's what real friends are for." said Kenny.

After meeting with Kenny, Michael had contacted Janice, Sarah, Regina, and the other patients that had allegedly been sexually harassed by Patricia at her Practice. He couldn't believe that there were twenty-two complaints against her. Although he really loved her, and he was hurt, he was glad that he would be divorced from her soon.

Michael's phone rang several times before he could answer it, and it was Yolanda. He had no idea what she wanted.

"Hello," he answered.

"Hi Michael, its Yolanda," Michael paused.

"Ahh, I'm sure I'm the last person you want to talk to, but I have some information that I need to share with you" said Yolanda.

FOR LOVE OR MONEY?

"What information, haven't you shared enough?"

"I realize that I hurt you by sleeping with your wife, and I'm sorry, but I have to tell you some things that could help you later."

Michael said "Okay, talk."

So, Yolanda replied in one big breath.

"Well, a while back Patricia came to my house after a bad day at work, and she began to tell me about a patient that she had always had a crush on, how she touched all over her breast during an examine, and how she stuck her hand into her vagina without gloves on."

"Okay, and…?"

"Well, Michael she even openly admitted to me how she had done this to several other patients in the past and how much she loved women, but she was afraid to tell you and I thought you should know."

Michael was quiet and finally replied after mentally taking all this in.

"Okay, umm so what's in it for you Yolanda?"

"Nothing, I figured it was the least I could do," said Yolanda.

"I thought ya'll were best friends as well as lovers?" said Michael.

"We were, I just thought I could help you after the damage I've done" said Yolanda.

"Well, if I can get you to send a written statement addressed to me at my office what you just explained to me that would be very helpful" said Michael.

Yolanda was trying to destroy as much of Patricia's life as she possibly could. She never got over that argument that they had, and never forgave Patricia, plus she was always envious of her marriage. So she made sure the least little thing Patricia did she would use it against her.

"Okay, what's the mailing address?" said Yolanda.

Michael gave Yolanda his work address, and even though he was pissed at her low down dirty ways he thanked her for the information she'd just revealed. He knew it would help his divorce case, and sexual harassment case that he was building against his unfaithful and greedy wife.

Months and months had gone by and finally their court date had arrived. Michael was excited that the drama was about to end. He represented himself and was very well prepared to begin. Patricia showed up with her Attorney, dressed in a Kenneth Cole navy blue suit, matching diamond earrings, tennis bracelet set, and designer high heels that Michael had bought her when they were madly in love. He had lavished her with so many gifts that she would probably never meet another man that will do those things for her that Michael did, and she knew it. She gazed her eyes over at Michael, hoping he would be looking at her but he wasn't. He was in deep concentration regarding what he needed to do legally to get this skank outta his life for good.

The Judge began the divorce proceeding, and the sexual harassment case followed shortly. He wanted both cases to be heard while all of his witnesses were willing to testify. He started with Patricia. Patricia's Attorney had asked for one million dollars in damages, the house, the Porsche, and Alimony for the duration of their marriage. Five of Dr. Brown's older patients testified that she was a great Doctor and that they have never seen or heard such nonsense! They all raved about Patricia's work ethics, but unfortunately, they didn't know the real deal.

Renee got on the witness stand and testified against Michael. She told the court what she saw the night of Michael's Birthday Party. Laura, Patricia's little sister was there for support only. She had no idea what to believe. She was always the perfect little peacemaker. She just knew her marriage wasn't in trouble and she didn't like rocking anyone else's boat.

After the Judge heard Patricia's case, and the testimonies, the Judge announced that they would reconvene after lunch and he bang his gavel. Everyone in the Courtroom gathered their belongings and took a lunch break. Patricia sashayed out of the courtroom, and stumbled against the table as she rolled her eyes at everyone who she thought was beneath her.

Michael was excited that he had everybody that was held accountable on his side. They all showed up as promised ready, willing and able to testify. Kenny was there, rubbing his hands together, as if he were nervous, willing and ready to tell what he knew. Along with Michaels' unveiled new love Maria. Janice and her husband were there. She was nervous as usual, but just wanted justice. She had never been more humiliated in her life. Yolanda was so ashamed that she sat in the back of the court in disguise with a blond wig on. She knew all of her dirt was about to come out too. Sarah and Regina were there and ready to testify as well, even if it meant their jobs, along with ten of the twenty-two women that had been sexual harassed, and assaulted by Dr. Brown over the years.

Once the court reconvened, everyone took his or her place. The Judged called Kenny to the witness stand. Kenny explained what he saw the night Patricia and Yolanda were in his nightclub. He explained that he saw Yolanda's hand up Patricia's dress, and how they were engaged in kissing, and hugging each other and they had went into a private room for hours. He explained how he secretly followed them into the private room, and grabbed his camera to take a picture of them in this sexual act. And, the Judge was writing notes.

"Okay, will that be all Sir?" said the Judge.

"Yes, sir" said Kenny.

"Thank you for your testimony, you may step down now," said the Judge.

Kenny walked down off the witness stand looking directly at Patricia squirming in her seat in disbelief of what he saw and that the photos came from Kenny! She thought, *That asshole set me up! I knew I saw a flash one night, but I had no idea what it was or who did it.*

Michael said, "I'd like to call my next witness to the stand please Judge."

"Yes, you may."

"I'd like to call Miss Maria Vasquez to the witness stand."

Maria had no idea that Michael would call her to testify against Patricia. Maria got up slowly, very well dressed. Patricia looked at her as if she saw herself. Patricia had never seen Maria dressed so well, she felt cloned. And she wondered where she got the money to buy such an elegant dress, and wearing shoes that were not run over. Michael examined her on the stand.

"So, Miss Maria can you tell the court who you are and what you observed in the Brown family?"

Maria didn't have to clear her throat anymore. She was comfortable with Michael. Patricia couldn't understand how the dirty, unsure, uneducated little Maria could speak so well in front of a Judge and a room full of people. Patricia thought she sounded and appeared so educated, and successful.

"Well, I am Maria Vasquez and I was The Browns' housekeeper a few days a week. And he worked very hard to be sure their household was cared for. When he wasn't working he was at home waiting on his wife to come home most weekends. I also observed that she would stay out for nights at a time, and he would be at home calling and waiting for her the next morning."

FOR LOVE OR MONEY?

The Judge stated and asks "you are a very young and pretty intellectual woman, so how did Dr. Brown treat you Miss Maria?"

"She treated me awful. She was rude most days, and hateful. She treated me as if I were an uneducated slave. But she had no idea that I had my Bachelor's Degree in Sociology and my Master's Degree in Psychology."

"So, why were you a Housekeeper?' ask the Judge.

Maria explained to the court that she couldn't find employment, and had to do housework just to have income coming in.

"Did Mrs. Brown ever make sexual advances towards you?" Ask Mr. Brown.

"No, sir, she did not directly. However, she did get undressed in front of me on many occasions while I was cleaning, and she was naked getting dressed for an event or for an evening out with her friends."

"Okay that'll be all Ma'am, thank you."

"You may step down, your next witness Mr. Brown." said the Judge.

Michael called his next witness to the stand.

"Your Honor, I'd like to call Mrs. Janice L. Woods to the witness stand."

Janice proceeded to get up. Her husband patted her on the shoulder to let her know he was there for moral support. Janice's legs were trembling, and she tripped on the thick courtroom floor carpet as she walked up the three tiny steps.

"Are you okay madam," asks the officer.

"Yes, thank you." said Janice in a trembling voice.

FOR LOVE OR MONEY?

And she sat down slowly on the witness stand; she took a deep breath hoping that this would be short and wishing that she didn't have to go thru this. But she knew if she didn't Dr. Brown would continue this unwanted, violating, and unprofessional behavior towards other patients. So she knew she had to take a stand for herself, and others.

Michael asks Janice "What is your relationship to the Doctor?"

"She is my Gynecologist."

"How long had you been her patient?

"I've been going to her for a little over a year" said Janice.

Patricia's Attorney interjected and he shouted thru the courtroom like a child on a playground.

"Your Honor if she's been going to her over a year, and she never experienced this so- called unwanted behavior with Doctor Brown, why is she making false allegations now, and continuing seeing her?"

"Overruled" you may proceed questioning Mr. Brown," said the Judge.

"Thank you Your Honor" said Michael.

Michael then asks, "Mrs. Woods on the day in question, what were you being seen for?"

"It was my annual pap check up." Janice replied, rubbing her sweaty palms together, and lightly patting her feet on the floor.

"Okay can you tell me what happened?" said Michael.

"Yes sir. The PA called me back to the exam room and she prepped me for my pap smear. She told me to get undressed so that the Dr. could examine me. So, I did. And then she said the Doctor will be in to

64

see you shortly, and she exited the room. I got up onto the examining table, and put the white sheet over my body. And the door opened suddenly, and it was Dr. Patricia Brown."

"And what did she say or do?" ask Michael.

"She ask me how I was doing, and told me to lay back, and spread my legs and she helped me put my feet into the stirrups, so I did, that was normal."

Patricia's Attorney abruptly interjected again and said "but if you were uncomfortable with the PA not in the room, and it was standard procedure for her to accompany the Doctor, why did you lie on the table and open your legs? Isn't it true that you wanted an attractive, prominent, wealthy Doctor to notice you? And to come on to you Mrs. Woods while you were undressed alone in the office? Mrs. Woods you wanted her to touch you didn't you? Or you would have waited for the PA to come back into the room!"

The Judge banged his gavel, and said **'YOU ARE OUT OF ORDER",** and everyone in the courtroom booed Patricia's Attorney.

"Please be quiet and respect my Courtroom or your case will be dismissed!"

"Yes, sir your Honor" and he took his seat.

Everyone in the Courtroom was so surprised by Patricia's Attorneys' sudden out burst. The courtroom was loud, and Yolanda was laughing hysterically. She loved drama, and had no real life of her own. She was just there to destroy Patricia's life, what was left of it.

Laura and her husband were just observing this mess, and couldn't believe this was happening. Renee was looking around wondering and wishing she could have gotten the $100,000 that she tried to extort from Michael earlier. She had no idea that he'd gotten it, and he waited for her that day at the Park, but she missed out on it sitting in jail on the account of she didn't have a driver's license from a speeding violation.

Wiggling impatiently, Sarah and Regina couldn't wait to hear the rest. They knew something was wrong at work, because the clientele had dwindled, business was getting slower, and people were complaining. Kenny was happy that his testimony was over, and Maria just wanted some peace. Janice's husband wanted to jump out of his seat to defend his wife, but he knew he would be held in contempt of court if he did. So, he maintained his cool.

As Michael rubbed the palm of his hands, looking across the room, and stood tall he said, "May I continue Your Honor?"

"Yes, you may."

"Okay Janice, after you noticed that the PA wasn't in the room what happened?"

"The Doctor took the cover off of me, and began massaging my breast in an unusual, sexual way."

"Did you like it?" ask Michael.

"No sir, I did not."

"Okay continue." Michael said.

"And then she told me to lie back, and put my feet in the stirrups, relax and close my eyes. Once I lay back, and opened my legs, she inserted her fingers into my vaginal area without gloves on."

"How did you know she didn't have gloves on if the cover was over you obstructing your sight from seeing her hands?" said the Judge.

"Because there's a different feeling, a warmer, slicker feeling than if a cold, tough surgical glove was used" replied Janice.

"Okay, and then what did you do?" ask Michael.

The courtroom was quiet, and Patricia looked humiliated and her face was beginning to bead with sweat. Her attorney was mad because the Judge kept overruling him when he tried to defend her.

"After she began to grope and rub on me, I said what in the hell do you think you're doing Doctor? I frantically said stop, and I jumped up off the table, grabbed my dress, purse and ran out of the exam room. As I was running, I ran into the PA in the Hallway, and she tried to ask me what happened, but I kept running."

"Okay, thank you for your testimony Mrs. Woods," said the Judge.

"That will be all Your Honor," said Michael.

Michael then called Sarah, Dr. Brown's Physician Assistant to the stand. Patricia was giving her the eye, as if she could intimidate her from telling the truth. The Judge asks her what she knew. Sarah explained that she saw Janice running from Dr. Brown's exam room in utter shock, with tears streaming down her face. Her dress was on backwards, and she had on one shoe.

"I ask Dr. Brown what had happened and she stated that the patient was upset because she just found out she had a sexual transmitted disease, which was a lie," said Sarah.

"And then Dr. Brown told me that I could go home since she was the last patient on that particular Friday, so I did. When I got downstairs I saw Mrs. Woods sitting in the lobby in tears. And I ask her was she okay, and she told me what had just happened. I told her to go into the rest room and wash her face, and put her dress on correct, and she did. I then hung around to make sure she got into her car safe, and gave her my number for moral support."

"Well, you sound like a great person to have around in a crisis" said the Judge.

FOR LOVE OR MONEY?

"I'd like to think so" said Sarah.

"Well, you may step down Miss Sarah," said the Judge.

Sarah stepped down nervously, and she was afraid to look over at Dr. Patricia, her boss who she had just ratted on! She knew things would never be the same professionally between the two of them. And she knew it would be hard in the office environment, so she'd better start looking for another job soon.

The next witness was Regina, she explained to the court that she saw the San Diego Deputy come to the office, and serve Dr. Brown papers.

"Is that all you observed" said the Judge.

"Yes, sir", and just that the entire office had been noticing irrational behavior in Dr. Brown lately and we were all getting complaints about her."

"Okay Miss Regina, thank you, you may step down."

Regina had to walk slowly, because she had on six-inch heels that made her look like a hooker. A cheap plastic mini skirt, a midriff top, a red wig, three inch acrylic nails on that were freshly painted with fake diamond studs in them, with big droopy cheap earrings on, a nose ring, lots of arm bangles, and a cheap bright yellow scarf around her neck. The people in the courtroom (even the Judge) just shook their heads in disbelief that she had the nerves to come to court dressed like a hooker!

Michael called Renee to the witness stand last. Michael asks Renee several questions about her relationship with her sister Patricia. And he asks her one last question.

"Renee is it true that you tried to extort $100,000 dollars from me to cover up a false accusation that I was sleeping with our Housekeeper just to break up my marriage to your sister?"

She licked her lips, and paused, as he pulled out the cashier's check that he had for her written out in her name. The key word was "sleeping with", because Michael was a great Lawyer, and he knew he had to word it just right, it was for him "kissing her", but he couldn't say that in court under oath, it would have back fired against him.

"Miss Renee, remember you are under oath," said the Judge. Plus she was too scared to lie in court.

Renee said, "Yes, I did."

"Thank you," said Michael.

"Miss Renee you may step down" said the Judge.

"Mr. Brown will that be all of your witness's sir?" asks the Judge.

"Yes, your Honor it is, But, I'd like to thank the Court for hearing our cases Your Honor," said Michael. He knew just what to say to earn any Judges respect.

"You are most welcome; you may take your seat Mr. Brown," said the Judge.
Patricia's Attorney jumped up, and called the remainder of the witnesses they had which were the old ladies that really had no idea what was going on to testify. They all raved about Patricia, and had no sexual abuse allegations against her because they weren't her type. She liked much younger women; old women just didn't turn her on.

After a long day of many testimonies, the Judge went back to deliberate. After carefully reviewing both cases, the Judge had reached a decision. Patricia lost everything. He granted their divorce, and he ruled that Patricia gets her own clothes and anything that she brought into the marriage. I got to keep the glass house that I had built, which was our primary resident. I got to keep my Porsche, all of my money, boat, condo, and everything that was in our home. She left with her Mercedes, jewelry, and nothing but the clothes on her back. We all jumped for joy and I thanked all of my witnesses for a job well done! Maria walked up to Michael and kissed him on the lips, and looked at Patricia standing next to her Attorney, and pointing to Maria.

Patricia said "Is this what you've been seeing?" And, Maria spoke up with confidence finally.

"Yes, I have been seeing Michael, but we never slept together. I have too much class for that, now go get your things and get your trifling ass out of our house! And furthermore, now who's uneducated, have no skills, doesn't know how to dress, and have run over shoes?" Maria said with a smirk on her face.

Patricia was pissed, and grabbed her things, and said, "You haven't seen the last of me bitch!" and walked out.

Maria felt good for finally being able to have the guts to stand up to Patricia after all the humiliation she'd put her thru over the years. Everyone had gathered outside the courthouse, and wished each other well. Patricia saw her Sister, Renee standing to the side.

"I had no idea that you knew Michael was seeing the Maid, and you tried to keep it from me by extorting money from Michael, you dirty broad" said Patricia, turning up her nose at Renee.

"Well, if you would have paid him more attention, you wouldn't have lost your husband to the maid!" said Renee.

And Renee walked away got into her car and drove off. Sweet little Laura and her husband were speechless. They didn't know what to say.

"Call me if you need me okay" said Laura.

"Okay, baby sis," said Patricia. Laura grabbed her husband's hand and they walked away from all the drama and went home.

FOR LOVE OR MONEY?

Patricia's Attorney was disappointed that he lost their case; he knew the pictures of Dr. Brown engaged sexually with Yolanda messed up their defense. He had no idea that they had pictures as proof, Patricia never told him about those. But he murmured to her.

"We will talk later okay?" The outraged Attorney said.

Patricia just rolled her eyes at him, lit a cigarette and he walked away. But she knew he would send her a bill soon. He had spent many hours and days trying to defend her. She was devastated that she was exposed, lost her husband and her case!

Michael and Maria walked down the stairs and just starred into each other's eyes. They were happy that his divorce was granted, and he got to keep everything he had worked so hard for. Maria was thinking, *"Thank God I don't have to work for her anymore"*. They walked to the car and Michael reached out to open the car door for Maria. As she got into her car, Michael asks her to follow him home to the Condo. It wasn't such a good idea for them to go back to his main house, after all his divorce was only final a few hours ago.

Maria followed Michael to his Condo off the Coast, and they grabbed a bite to eat (just before they arrived) at a popular little Italian Restaurant on the Boulevard. They were hungry, and it had been a long day in Court, they just wanted to eat, relax and go to the Condo. Maria ordered soup and salad with diet coke. Michael had Lasagna with breadsticks, and a salad. Michael ordered them both a glass of dinner wine to toast a new beginning.

"Here's to us Maria", said Michael.

And they touched their glasses together smiling at each other as if it was their first date. Once they finished eating, Michael paid the bill; left the waitress a hefty tip, and they got into their cars and drove to the Condo. Maria parked her car in the guest parking, and Michael drove his Porsche into his one-car garage. Maria got out and waited on Michael to gather his things, and offered to help carry something.

71

FOR LOVE OR MONEY?

"Oh, no thanks baby, you're resting tonight."

They both walked up the stairs, as Maria led, and Michael sat his briefcase down, held his other belongings in the other arm, and opened the door.

"You may enter darling," said Michael with charisma. And she walked thru the door proud.

"Have a seat sweetheart" and she pulled off her linen jacket, walked slowly, and sat on the sofa.

"I'll be right back Maria; I'm going to take a hot shower. Would you like to join me?" He asks.

"Why, yes, I'd be delighted to. I could use a good hot shower," said Maria. *Damn* she thought he'd never ask!

Michael turned on the water for their shower, and he watched Maria get undressed. He just sat in the chair in the bedroom, and watched her take off each piece of clothing piece by piece, and admired her. He helped her take off her shoes, and assisted her in the shower.

"Here, get in, be careful not to slip and fall," said Michael, touching her body softly.

"I won't" said Maria, grinning from one side of her face to the other.

He washed Maria's hair, back, and breast area first. And then he went down to her arms, hands, and legs. Then he washed her feet! Michael had a foot fetish. He loved washing his woman's body, especially her feet. He simply enjoyed pampering his lady. He began kissing all over her face, and body. He grabbed a brush from a shelf that was over the shower, and brushed her hair gently.

Once they finished showering, he turned off the water, helped her get out, and he then dried her body off. He blow-dried her silky black hair, after he rubbed her soft body in African oil. She was so relaxed, and had always wanted to experience this, and finally the day came thanks to Patricia!!! They were both tired, but made passionate love to each other finally!

Michael, and Maria had cuddled all night, and he hated parting with her. They watched the sunrise together coming from the shore. They had the windows open, and you could hear the birds chirping, feel the wind blowing, and the waves pounding on the seashore. Maria got up, and went into the bathroom to wash up, and she grabbed a towel, and underneath it was a huge ring!

"Ohhhhh", Michael, what's this?" she said surprised!

He was standing in the arched doorway, smiling at her, with no shirt on, looking as sexy as hell, and he took her by the hand, got on his knee in front of her, and he looked up at her.

"I know I just got a divorce, but I'm in love with you. Maria, I love you because you're always here for me when no one else is. You're sensitive, and caring towards me as well as to others. I love the way you laugh, and your glowing smile finds my soul. I feel your peace when you are asleep. I love seeing you when you first wake up, it gives me hope. I love how you comfort me, you're my Angel. I love that you're the last person I see at the end of the day, and I never want to lose that, will you marry me?"

Tears fell down Maria's face, and he touched one as if it were shimmering gold!

"Oh, yes Michael, I will marry you, I love you too!

"Do you have any idea how long I've waited to hear that?" said Michael.

He placed the huge diamond ring on her finger, and they embraced each other with such a passion that no one could change their hearts.

FOR LOVE OR MONEY?

Maria was so excited that for once in her life she was going to marry the man of her dreams! She had no idea that it would be the man she used to work for.

"I told you that you wouldn't be a maid long, didn't I? Didn't I?" He said with great enthusiasm.

"Yes, Michael, you did tell me that."

"Maria I've been in love with you for a while now, but I didn't know how to express it, because I was married to Patricia."

Michael knew if he had committed adultery, he would have lost half of everything to Patricia. Now that Maria was going to wed Michael, a prominent Attorney, she had to get herself together. She knew all his friends knew her as the "Maid". But, now she would be proudly introduced as his fiancé. She was nervous about that, and about everyone thinking that she stole Michael from Patricia and that they were sleeping together before his divorce. Maria was just the caring type, and she cared what other people thought about her character.

Weeks and weeks had gone by, and Maria wasn't working anywhere, Michael was busy as usual. And they would meet up for lunch still at the Condo.

"Hey Maria, when do you want to move your things in here?" ask Michael.

"So, soon?" she asks.

"Won't everybody be suspicious; it's only been a few weeks since your divorce?"

"Listen babe, I don't give a damn what everybody thinks. They don't pay my bills, and they don't make me feel the way you make me feel, so to hell with them."

"Well, I just thought about your reputation, that's all," said Maria.

"You are too kind and considerate, that's why I love you. Now go get your things, and move in with me, you're my lady right?"

"Well…" she paused.

"Well, what?" said Michael.

"There's something you should know about me, said Maria.

"Okay, what's that, I'm sure it can't be all that bad," said Michael

"Well, I have breast Cancer, and the Doctor says I won't live any more than one or two more years, it's in its last stage."

"Wow, Maria why didn't you tell me this? Oh, honey I'm so sorry," said Michael.

"I didn't tell you because I wanted you to love me for me, not because you felt sorry for me."

"Are you getting the best care possible?" asks Michael. And he grabbed her hands in the palm of his hands.

"Yes, I am. Please don't worry about me, lets just enjoy each day together okay?"

"Okay, I'll try not to worry, but you know I will," said Michael.

Three Months had gone by, and as usual Michael was at work earning that money. He stopped a moment to look out the window, and then his phone rang. Patricia called Michael at work.

And he answered. "Good day Michael Brown Attorneys' Office how may I assist you?"

FOR LOVE OR MONEY?

"Hey it's me, Patricia, you got a minute to talk to me?" sounding desperate.

"What is it Patricia?"

"Do you miss me?" said Patricia.

"Look Patricia, we were together for years, and I treated you like a Queen. I gave you everything a woman could ask for, and you cheated, so deal with the consequences, and quit calling me!"

Patricia sighed, "Hmmm, so how long have you been sleeping with the Maid?"

"Are you referring to Maria?" Michael asks, and Patricia was silent.

"I didn't make love to her until after our divorce. We were strictly platonic, because I valued our marriage, but apparently you didn't."

"Well, I have something to tell you?" said Patricia.

"What Patricia?"

"Would you meet me this evening at the Diner down the street from our house at 6:00?" said Patricia

"I am busy this evening, maybe another time." And Michael hung up the phone.

The evening was getting late, and Michael had left the office and went to the Condo. He was now preparing another case he had been working on and paying bills. Maria was still unpacking her things, but she didn't feel too well. She had unpacked the last of her things at Michael's Condo. Maria was now wearing a 5K-diamond ring, and was beginning to plan their wedding.

"Hey honey, how are you?" asks Michael.

"Oh, I'm fine; but I don't feel too good today." replied Maria.

Michael was in his office at home, but he put down his pen to tend to Maria.

"What can I get you babe?" ask Michael.

"Nothing, I'm okay, really."

"Okay, well, let me know if you need anything."

"I will, don't worry" said Maria.

"Oh, hey, by the way, guess who called me today after three months of silence?"

"Who?" said Maria?

"Patricia" said Michael.

Maria's eyes got really big, and her heart started pounding, thinking that he wanted her back.

"Oh, what did she want"? Ask Maria.

"She wanted to know if I missed her and if I still loved her, and I said "no."

"Oh yeah, did my name come up?"

"Yeah, it did," said Michael.

"What did she say?"

"She asks me how long we'd been sleeping together?"

"And what did you say?"

FOR LOVE OR MONEY?

"I told her that we didn't make love until after our divorce. And she was quiet, but then she asks me to meet her today."

"So did you meet her?" said Maria.

"No baby, I didn't, she said she had something to tell me. But I didn't care; I wasn't falling for her trap."

"Hmm, that's weird. Well I'm going to go lay down a few minutes, and then I'll get up and do some magazine shopping for our wedding".

"You believe me right?" ask Michael.

"Yes, I do believe you Michael."

"Oh, hey you don't have to do anything, let's get a wedding planner." Michael replied.

"No thanks Michael, a real woman plans her own wedding."

"Alright baby, whatever you want just get it". Michael suggested.

And Maria gave Michael a kiss on the cheek and walked into the bedroom to lie down. Michael was preparing for the next case, which was taking its toll on him after the divorce, and sexual harassment case for Janice. So, he spent a lot of time at work and in his home office after hours.

Patricia felt so depressed that she had to medicate herself with antidepressants. She drank a lot, so towards the end of her career she rarely showed up for work. Sarah and Regina both had quit. They put their two weeks' notice in shortly after her court case. The Class Action Lawsuit against Dr. Brown just overwhelmed her and the fact that she lost her husband, and now this, losing her Medical License. Patricia's world was falling apart. The life she once had with Michael was peaceful, loving, caring, and giving, but it all came from him. She knew now that she truly took her husband for granted. All the trips, romance, and gifts he gave her would be missed, and she knew that

Maria would be getting those things she once had. All she knew is that it wouldn't be her anymore.

Before the divorce, Michael no longer took time out to call her, take her out, cook for her, buy her things, or even make love to her. The last time they were intimate was several months ago. He showed no concern for her at all. Even though Yolanda never testified against her in court, she had lost her friendship. Patricia tried to amend their friendship, but it was never the same. Kenny at the club didn't express the VIP treatment when she did show up at his club with run down guest at her side. As a Matter of fact, he asks her to leave one night, because she was too drunk, and she didn't have enough money to pay for the drinks she had already drunk.

Patricia could hardly see to drive home, after Kenny had kicked them outta his night club for not being able to pay. The run-down looking guy and girl that she was with had to drive her home. The guy drove her Mercedes, and the girl drove her own car. Patricia was renting a one-bedroom apartment on the lower end of town, an area she'd always despised. Even as a Physician she had always blown all of her money. She would buy senseless items that she knew she didn't need. Give countless money to her so-called friends; she pretty much took care of Yolanda. Yolanda didn't work for years because she knew Patricia would pay her way. But where were all of them now that she needed them?

Once they arrived at Patricia's apartment, they carried her in. She was too drunk to even know who brought her home. After they dumped her on the sofa, they began rummaging thru her things, and taking what they wanted. The girl took Patricia's wedding ring out of her jewelry box, her pearl necklace, and many other expensive items. The guy took her DVD player, DVD's, CDs, they went thru her purse, but there was no cash. So, they took her credit cards (which all of them were cancelled by Michael), and most of her designer clothes and handbags. Patricia knew they were the scum of the earth, yet she hung out with them in her moment of despair.

FOR LOVE OR MONEY?

When she woke up the next morning, she realized she had nothing. She actually thought she had been robbed, because they left her apartment door wide open. But there was no sign of forced entry.

Patricia called the Police, and reported her items missing. However, she wasn't able to get them back, or file it under her insurance, because she had not paid her premium in months, so she no longer had coverage. Prestigious Patricia decided to sell her Mercedes, and the few designer clothes she had left (after being robbed) to pay for her rent and get food. She didn't want to tell her sisters, especially Renee, because she'd just make her feel worse. Plus she didn't want anyone to know how terrible she was doing since her divorce from Michael. She didn't call Laura, because she knew all perfect little Laura would say is *"Just Pray."*

Patricia was at the bottom of the pit. She could no longer afford the lavish lifestyle she once led, so she sold her Mercedes for a small amount of cash out of desperation. She took the cab to her job so that she could continue to earn some money. Her $1,500.00 dollar a month rent was due in a few days on her apartment, but she didn't have it. Unfortunately, she was already three months behind, and facing an eviction. And even though she had just sold her Mercedes, she needed that money for survival. Patricia never imagined that she would be looking out at the world from a poor helpless person's eyes. She was used to the finer things in life. Even though her parents grew up struggling, she was never hungry or homeless. However, she'd met the man of her dreams, and didn't have to want for anything. She was a successful Physician, who was about to hit rock bottom, and now that her career and lifestyle was on the line, she wasn't sure how long she'd have the *"Dr. Title".*

The summer time was at its end, autumn passed and the winter months had come. The trees were naked, and the beach days were at an end. All the summer parties were over, lying out on the beach for hours, the warm sun beaming on your back, swimming, and the outdoors picnics. Although living on the West Coast it didn't get too cold. But some of the outdoors activities would soon cease for a short time, and there would be little beach activity for a season.

FOR LOVE OR MONEY?

The sexual harassment case was a nightmare memory for Dr. Brown, which was yet the biggest challenge she had faced. Something she lost over her promiscuous behavior. She'd jeopardized her career to full-fill her own sexual desires, and she jeopardized her marriage to sleep around with her no good, jealous friend Yolanda, who didn't want her to have Michael from jump.

Patricia had a flash back, she'd remembered that her fine ass patient Janice was twirling her thumbs, and nervous on the witness stand. She knew Michael had represented Janice quite well, as he does all of his clients. She was also hurt because her Attorney quit; she never paid him for her divorce case. But embarrassed enough, she had been appointed a Public Defendant, some new guy that recently became a Lawyer who cared less if she won or not. Once the Judge heard Janice's case from Michael, and the defense team was weak, the Judge didn't waste any time deliberating, and Janice won her case. All of the other patients that were sexually abused by Dr. Brown had testified, and all of their testimonies were the same. They all stated in their testimonies that *"Patricia would wait until the PA was out of the exam room to make her move."*

She knew the Judge would order that she have her License revoked. She didn't know what to do anymore, because she lost her Medical License, and would never be able to Practice Medicine again. She had nothing to take, no property, and no money. She'd remembered Michael looking at her and shook his head back and forth in disgust.

She remembered Maria just looked at her when they were dismissed, and said, *"Now who's uneducated, have no skills, doesn't know how to dress, and have run over shoes?"* And Maria just walked away. Holding her head up high, and Michael walked right behind her. Patricia had burst out in tears. She had no support from anyone.

Dr. Patricia Brown was no longer an OBGYN; she had no practice, no medical license, no money, no house, no car, and no husband, not even a friend. As the mental video played in her head, she thought about her ex-maid walking off with her handsome ex-husband. She was so hurt, and she felt like her life was at an end.

As time passed, she heard it thru the grapevine that Michael had proposed to Maria the night of her divorce. No matter what, Michael would no longer give Patricia the time of day. She had nowhere to live because she was evicted from her apartment, no food, no car, no clothes, so she turned to prostitution. Although she knew better, because of her precarious position, she had to get some money somehow. She tried on various occasion to call him, but he wouldn't take her calls any longer. Patricia needed to talk to Michael desperately to let him know that she was pregnant. Even though she was pregnant by Michael, she knew her situation still wouldn't change his mind about how he felt about her now. He had always wanted a child, but she was taking birth control pills, pretending that she just hadn't conceived yet. She made Michael spend thousands of dollars on test to see what was preventing them from getting pregnant, but Michael had no clue that she was deceiving him all those years. Patricia never wanted a child, because it was too much work, and it would take the attention that Michael gave her away and the focus would be on the baby. He never really knew how selfish Patricia was until now.

After Patricia lost all she ever had, she had no one to call on. So, she gathered up enough change from strangers on the street and caught the bus downtown in search of anything she could get a hold of, food, a warm place to lay, etc. It was getting late, and she was tired, hungry and cold. She was under a bridge and some men drove up and ask her if she needed help. She said *"yes"*. So, she got into the car with three strange men thinking that they were going to help her and they all took turns beating her up, and rapping her. Once they were finished with her, they took her back to the bridge and dumped her out of their car.

She was beaten pretty bad, bruised, her face and nose was bleeding, she began to regurgitate. Patricia hadn't eaten in a few days, and she had no idea how she would get food. It was raining, and she needed shelter or help from just being beat up and rapped. She smelled like fish, her clothes were soiled, her hair was matted to her head, and her breath could knock a door off of its hinges. She had her head down, and she was beat up so bad (in desperate need of medical attention) that she was unrecognizable. Later that dark cold night, she met a woman who walked underneath the bridge that offered her somewhere to stay.

"Hi ma'am, you need some help?" said a familiar voice. Patricia slowly raised her head, and got up, looked up at the woman, and it was Yolanda.

Dirty and Unrecognizable, "Hi Yolanda, it's me, Pat."

"Oh, my God, what are you doing out here? Pat what happened to you?" said Yolanda.

Clearing her throat, "Mmmm, I was beat up a few days ago, rapped by three men, and they dumped me under this bridge."

"Well that's what you get, I hired them with your money to do that to you bitch. Now you see how it feels to have nothing!"

"Plus I heard the Maid got yo' man!!!" said Yolanda, and she laughed and walked away.

Patricia cried after she ran into her ex-best friend, Yolanda, and the way she set her up to be beaten and sexually assaulted. She began walking in the rain, she felt hopeless, and she ran across a small house on the corner that had people running in and out. It was a dope house. *"What do I have to lose",* she thought so she went inside, and began smoking cocaine with strangers. Her dress had blood on it, but she had no idea because she was so high she didn't care anymore, besides the drugs took away her hunger and her problems.

Patricia's family had been looking for her for quite some time. They even called Michael to see if he had heard from her and no one knew anything of her whereabouts. Patricia was now nine months pregnant and officially homeless. At nine months pregnant, she still tried to prostitute in hopes of making a little money, but none of the tricks wanted to be with her. So, she got in where she fit in, the dope house. She hadn't tried to contact anyone in her family, not even Michael.

Maria had planned a very elegant, yet simple local wedding. She planned it in town at her church, so that all of her family and friends could come. Michael had won another case, and was on vacation for a month. He needed the time off for the wedding, plus he had been working perversely over the past few months. He was driving thru town one day, and saw Yolanda at a local coffee shop.

"Hey Michael, how are you?"

"Oh, hey Yolanda, I'm doing very well, how are you?" rolling his eyes.

"I'm doing okay," said Yolanda.

"Have you heard from Pat lately?"
"No, I've been busy working and getting ready for my wedding day."

"Wow, Congratulations, who's the lucky lady this time?"

"It's Maria."

"You're marrying the Maid?"

"Excuse me Yolanda, she's not a Maid, she's my fiancée and a soon to be an at-home wife." He said in a loud voice.

"Oh, great, so when and where is the big day?"

"It's at Hargrove Baptist Church, on the 25th of December."

"Nice, so you two are getting married on Christmas?"

"Yes, we are, because Maria is a gift."

FOR LOVE OR MONEY?

"Well, tell her I said CONGRATULATIONS! I gotta go," said Yolanda.

As soon as Yolanda left, Michael realized he shouldn't have told her anything about their wedding day. But it was too late now. He was certain that Yolanda would sure stir up something.

On the day of Maria's wedding, everything was perfect from the flowers, to her dress. Their nuptials began at 2 o'clock sharp. All of her family was there. Michael and his family were there. And she was nervous and just ready for it to be over, so that she and Michael could be together for once and for all. About half way thru the ceremony, Patricia showed up dirty, drunk, and high carrying (what appeared to be a gift) a wrinkled letter wrapped in a red ribbon. Her stomach was huge carry their baby in its last term. Everyone looked up with a huge surprise on their face.

"Oh, my God who is that?" murmured the crowd, pointing at Patricia.

Patricia still had some scars remaining from when she was taken away and beat up by those three men. The reverend ask, *"Is there anyone here that sees why these two should not be wed?"* All of a sudden, Patricia jumped up, and staggered to the altar, and she stood next to Michael, she looked at him, his eyes grew so big, and he knew how she found out about their wedding day, it was big mouth jealous ass Yolanda. And then Patricia said in a sluggish voice *"I do, and here's why"* She handed Michael the wrinkled letter, and pulled out a gun and shot herself in the head at the Altar.

All the guests in the pews got up and ran out of the church. The Reverend just stood there in shock. Maria started crying hiding behind Michael, which he had dived onto the floor by the podium. Maria had blood scattered all over her elegant white wedding gown, and Michael's face was full of Patricia's blood. After Patricia fell face forward on the carpet; Michael looked at Maria with tears in his eyes and asks her if she was alright. Maria was so shook up, she couldn't speak. So, he just held her in his arms. You could hear the sirens of the Paramedics and Police coming. Someone from the family had called 911 when they got up and ran outside the church.

FOR LOVE OR MONEY?

Although Michael knew Patricia was dead, Michael got up to see what condition she was in. He just starred at her, lying there in her blood. He took his coat jacket off and covered up her bruised and bloody face, and he looked at her stomach having no idea that she was pregnant. Michael thought *"could this have been why she wanted to talk to me a while back, and I ignored her?"* Michael just stood there and cried. He had no idea why Patricia did this. Maria was sitting on a pew in disbelief that this happened, wondering why she committed suicide, and how she knew when and where their wedding date was.

Michael looked at the bloody and wrinkled note that Patricia handed him, wrapped in a red ribbon, and it read:

My Dearest Michael:

Congratulations on your Wedding Day!

I had no idea that our lives would turn out like this and the past few months my life has been a mess. I want you to know that I did care about you, but I never loved you. I only married you for the money. I know that we were both successful in our careers, but I kept a secret from you for six years. I have been a lesbian all my life and I knew one day this would all come out, but not by me committing suicide. I thought by now I'd have most of your money and be gone to live with my lover Yolanda. Yolanda has always been a snake in the grass, but I loved her and her only. Shortly before you and I parted, I got pregnant by you. As you can see as I lie here before you at the altar on your wedding day; I am nine months pregnant with our child. Yolanda and I were going to raise our child without you. I never wanted to have a family with you, and I hated when you touched me, because I didn't love you, that's why I had been on birth control pills from the beginning of our relationship. You see Michael; all of this was premeditated from the beginning. And today is your lucky day; you get to bury your unborn child and me. You see we wouldn't have been in your life anyway. I hope you forgive me, if not do you think God will ever forgive me?

FOR LOVE OR MONEY?

Your Lesbian Ex-wife,
PAT

Michael's heart dropped, he began to weep even more, and he could not believe the audacity that Patricia would have the nerve to even do such a thing, and then to write a letter and committed suicide on his wedding day, especially in a church! Patricia was really selfish he thought. She pretended to love me, and cherish me all these years, and it was all a lie. She only wanted to be with me for the money.

Maria got off the pew and walked over to Michael, and she just held him in silence. She took her finger and wiped his eyes. The Police and Paramedics arrived at the church, and they walked in and ask what happened. Michael gave the bloody letter to the officer. The officer read the letter and began his investigation.

"Who is Yolanda?" asks the Officer.

Michael replied, "She was the deceased best friend and secret lover."

"Is she around here?" asks the officer.

"No sir" sniffling, said Michael.

"Do you know where we can locate her?"

"I can find out", said Michael"

"Okay, here's my card, contact me immediately when you find out her whereabouts." the Officer said.

Michael shook his head in agreement looking down at the floor. The Paramedics picked up Patricia and carried her bloody body out of the church on a stretcher strapped down, and covered with a lily-white sheet.

Maria wasn't feeling well after all that went down on their wedding day. The reverend and Maria's family were standing across

87

the street from the church waiting to see why Michael's Ex-wife, and her Ex-Boss committed suicide. Michaels' family wasn't surprised; they knew she was trouble from the beginning. But they never thought their marriage would end with one of them dead.

"What did that letter say?" ask Maria.

"She just told me that she kept a secret from me for six years, that she was a lesbian, how she never loved me, and that she was carrying my baby that I would never get to raise, and that she was in love with Yo-landa."

"Oh, wow, Michael, I'm so sorry."

"Well, Maria I'm sorry too" I'm sorry that I married a woman that I thought I knew but didn't. I'm sorry that she ruined our damn wedding day. Oh, Maria, I am so hurt."

"I know baby, me too. Lets postpone our wedding date until later" said Maria.

"Why should we allow Patricia's mistakes ruin our lives?" said Michael.

"I just think we should wait," said Maria wiping sweat and tears from Michael's face.

"Okay, but we are not going to wait too long Maria, I love you."

"I love you too Michael."

Michael had thanked all the guest who came and he reached in his wallet and paid all the servers, and services that they had hired, along with a hefty tip. And they got into the Porsche decorated with *"JUST MARRIED"* written all over it and went home.

Patricia's funeral was one week later. Michael didn't want to go, but he did out of respect for her and their unborn child. Maria was at his side as always. Renee and (her invisible husband) was there, her baby sister Laura and her husband was there comforting one another, and a host of other family members, friends, and co-workers. Unfortunately, Patricia's parents died a few years ago in a car accident coming home from vacation. A drunk driver hit them, and it killed them instantly. When the Eulogy was read, Laura was proud of all the accomplishments that Patricia had made. Renee was just waiting to see what all Patricia left her in the will. One of Patricia's friends sang a solo and everybody in the church cried. Nobody was sure if they were crying for their own salvation or Patricia's. But they did know that the soloist touched them.

Once the funeral was over, the pall barriers wheeled the casket outside, and Renee was the first one out the door. Yolanda showed up outside standing underneath a huge palm tree with a tight black dress on, wearing dark glasses, and waiting to get her cut.

"Why are you here?" ask Renee.

"She was my best friend," said Yolanda.

"Naw, all you did was turn her into a lesbian, and now look at what happened."

"Screw you bitch!" said Yolanda.

Renee walked up to Yolanda and slapped her in the face. She hit her so hard that her sunglasses flew off her face. Yolanda picked her glasses up, and charged towards Renee. They fought outside, and everybody stood by and watched. They had put the casket in the Hurst and were beginning to drive away.

Michael and Maria shook their heads in disbelief that they were fighting over what they thought they were going to get from Patricia. Once they arrived at the graveyard, everyone got out of their cars, and walked over to the site where Patricia would be buried. Michael and Maria took a seat. Laura and her husband sat next to Michael. All of the additional family and friends gathered around them, and the Pastor prayed. Renee showed up after the burial, because of the fight she had outside with Yolanda at the church.

Laura thanked everybody for coming to her sister's Home-Going, and she left in tears.

Finally, Yolanda showed up drunk after the majority of people were gone from the burial, poppin' off at the mouth.

"Well, the bitch is buried now; I guess she will burn in Hell." Michael just looked at her, and he grabbed her by the throat.

"Shut up, you are the reason all this happened."

"Michael stop, lets go, she's not worth it." Maria said. And they left the gravesite.

Drunk or sober, Yolanda loved to talk down about Patricia, even in her death. She had never forgiven Patricia for defending her marriage to Michael when they argued a year ago. Everyone was gone, and Yolanda put a yellow rose on Patricia's casket, and said *"here's to friends with money bitch!"* and walked away.

Kenny called Michael, while they were driving home. "Hey man, I just heard about Patricia, hey man I'm sorry."

"It's okay, man, hopefully, she'll be better off."

"She looked pretty bad man. I have no idea what happened to her in her last days, or what even drove her to suicide." said Michael.

"Yeah, when I heard she committed suicide at the church on your wedding day, I couldn't believe it." said Kenny.

"Yeah, and she was pregnant with my baby too."

"Awe Mike man, I'm really sorry to hear that, I know how much you wanted a child."

FOR LOVE OR MONEY?

"Yeah, I guess it wasn't in God's plan huh?" said Kenny.

"I guess not," said Michael

"Well, hang in there, and call me if you need anything, okay?"

"Okay" said Michael.

It was six months since Patricia had committed suicide. It was summer time again; Michael had remembered it was Patricia's favorite time of the year. He and Maria had moved into the glass house he had built for Patricia, but Maria had redecorated everything. Michael was outside planting a few flowers; something he'd always enjoyed doing, but didn't get to because Patricia always wanted to hire help, so he never got to enjoy gardening. Maria was inside cleaning up; she never thought she'd be looking out at the pool area, and it would one day be hers, after her and Michael got married. They were doing quite well. Patricia always thought Maria was a *"nobody"* and would never amount to anything because of her complacency as a maid, and her lack of education.

Maria was cleaning; she had found several pictures tucked away (in a flowered keep-sake box) far back in the hall closet of Patricia engaged with several other women. There were even notes she found where the women were begging Patricia to be her woman dated back when she was in her junior year in college. Maria thought, *"Apparently, she was popular but, I guess in the end, Patricia ended up with nobody"*. But she put them in the trash; she didn't want Michael to see them. He was already hurting enough.

While Maria was still cleaning out the closet, she began not to feel well, so she laid down. Michael was still outside planting flowers. Maria had already cooked dinner so that he wouldn't have to. She truly loved Michael, and she hoped he knew it and believed it was for all the right reasons. She always reassured him that she loved him and that her love for him was real. Maria had nothing to hide from him, and would never dream of hurting him the way that Patricia did.

After Michael finished in the yard, he walked inside and called for his fiancé. *"Maria, are you in here?"* said Michael. But Maria didn't answer. So, Michael walked up the stairs to see if Maria was in the bedroom. Maria was asleep on the king size bed, and had fallen asleep with Michael's picture in her arms. All he could do was smile, and he covered her up with a blanket, kissed her and closed the bedroom door. Michael went down stairs to see what Maria had cooked. He smelled the aroma thru the house. Maria was a good cook, and she was brought up to take care of the man. It was just her way of life. Now that she had someone to share her life with, even in her own sickness, she would be sure she'd done all the domestic things she knew every woman should do for her man. She submitted to Michael the way a woman should according to the bible. It didn't make her less of a person or a less of a woman, she just did what she knew was right. She enjoyed taking care of her man. Although, Michael wasn't used to that, it was him who did all the nice and thoughtful things. So, he really appreciated the kindness Maria's displayed in other ways.

Maria's health had been deteriorating but she didn't seem to let it faze her. She was in and out of the hospital and Michael had missed many days of work to take care of her. She was very independent, still trying to find a job to pull her own weight, take care of the house, plan their wedding day, and she'd hoped this time it would all turn out right. So, Michael and Maria both agreed on Saturday, August 5th for their wedding day.

It was the end of July, and the wedding plans were final, again. It was only one week from their wedding. The reverend decided not to charge Michael again after what had happened on Christmas Day with Patricia's unfortunate death. It was the last Friday before their wedding, and Michael had taken lots of pictures with Maria. They went to dinner and then he took her dancing. Both of them needed a little spice in their world since Maria had been ill and Michael's grievance. Michael and Maria went home at 2:00 A.M and they made love like it was their last time. But for Maria it always felt special with Michael. He knew just where to touch her, what to say and what to do. He was romantic, gentle, and he knew how to hold her afterwards. Michael was every woman's dream, but he was a one-woman man. After Maria fell asleep from being exhausted from making love to Michael all night long, he went down stairs to sign a document, and he sat it on the round coffee table. He felt very depressed, and overwhelmed with life, so he took some sleeping pills.

The next morning, Michael got up at 6 o'clock A.M (feeling a bit groggy) he took anti-depressants, and then he dragged himself into the kitchen to fix Maria's breakfast in bed and he placed a love letter on her breakfast tray underneath her napkin that read:

Maria,

Most men only get one time to truly love the women of their dream. I am fortunate enough to get two. Unfortunately, we both have been thru a lot, and I hope you get thru your illness soon. I want you to know that I am really hurting right now, and I just can't take it any-more. When you wake up my dear you will find me downstairs on the sofa, but my soul will be gone on with Patricia and my unborn child. She's whom I really love, and I can't find myself living without her. Please forgive me.

Love Michael

Maria woke up at about 10 o'clock A.M and found the break-fast tray aside her on the bed, and she smiled. The food had gotten cold, but she smiled at the thought of sweet Michael cooking her breakfast in bed. She turned on the flat screen T.V mounted on the wall, and she sat up on the bed to open the letter that Michael had writ-ten her. When she finished reading it, it wasn't the type of *"love letter"* that she expected, she said *"Oh, my God"* and ran downstairs to see what Michael was talking about. She saw him lying on the leather sofa, with his head drooped to the side, and an empty bottle of sleeping pills, and anti-depressants on the floor next to the sofa.

"Oh, Lord, what has he done?"

Maria called 911, and she began calling Michael's name, and shaking him trying to get him to wake up.

93

FOR LOVE OR MONEY?

"Michael, Michael wake up baby."

But she knew he had overdosed on the two bottles of pills. She could not believe he was so in love with Patricia that he would kill himself over her. He had just made love to her the night before like they would be together forever, and their wedding was only a few days away.

Once the Police arrived, Maria had already called her family to tell them what had happened to Michael, and the note he'd left her on her breakfast tray and they rushed right over. The Police took a statement from her, and the coroner covered and carried Michael's body away. Maria's Mother and sister arrived after the Police came, and they tried to comfort her as much as possible. They had just been thru this same tragedy just eight months ago with Michael's ex.

Maria told the Police what happened. Maria thought Michael was in love with her, and that he gave her no inclination that he still loved his ex-wife. Especially after he pretended he was so in love with her. All Maria's mom could do was listen. She didn't speak or comprehend much English; however, Maria had to translate in Spanish to her mom what was going on. She thought she was getting ready to marry the man that she had fallen in love with, but he was still in love with his deceitful deceased wife. For Maria, she loved Michael in her heart and soul. And no one in Maria's family had ever dated, or fell in love with a wealthy man. Senorita, Maria was the first.

When the police was leaving, he said *"call us if you need us Ma'am."*

Maria replied, *"Okay, I will Officer, thank you."*

And he placed his note-pad in his pocket, and he walked out the door.

Maria sat on the sofa, and gazed around the glass house. She couldn't believe that Michael took an overdose. She thought, *"Such a handsome, brilliant Attorney, he had a wonderful successful career, great friends, and co-workers, and this had to happen. But he deceived me just as Patricia did him, Hmmm. I didn't deserve any of this,"* cried Maria. She wiped her eyes with her bare hands until they were red and swollen. While her head was buried in her hands, her mom and sister comforted her.

"Mommy, he was going to marry me knowing that he didn't love me. I guess he really wanted to be with her. Why did he pretend with me? Why did he make love to me like I was the only one on his mind? What did I ever do to deserve this? How could he do this to me?" cried Maria.

All sorts of thoughts were racing thru her mind, and then she looked at the round table, and saw a document placed partially in an envelope that read *"Michael's Will."* She raised her head from her hands, and dried her weeping eyes and took the document off the table. Basilia, her Mom (which means Queen) and Adora her sister (Which means Adoration) was sitting on the opposite end of the sofa.

"What is that?" said Basilia.

"It appears to be some kind of legal document, "it looks like a will." Maria opened Michael's will and it read:

January 1, 2008

To My Dear Maria Vasquez:

Upon my death, I leave you all of my worldly possessions. I leave to Maria Vasquez my house, Condo, cars, money in all existing accounts (including business accounts), my business, boat, and any investments or savings that I possessed upon my death.

Please accept this Last Will and Testament as my last wishes.

Sincerely,
Mr. Michael Brown, Attorney

FOR LOVE OR MONEY?

A stream of tears fell from Maria's eyes. "Adora look at the date on this Will," said Maria.

"Michael knew he didn't want to live shortly after Patricia killed herself in December 2007."

"I see he sure didn't," said Adora.

"Oh, Maria I'm so sorry you have to experience this horror." But at least he thought enough of you to leave you something."

Maria could not grasp this whole incident. After all her wedding day with Michael her only love, were just a few days away.

Maria's mom and sister left after the coroner carried Michael's body away.

"Mom I'll talk with you later" said Maria, and they kissed one another goodbye.

Maria closed the glass door, stopped in the center of the floor, and looked around. She always wanted something nice, but she had no idea that she would own the home that she use to clean! She had no idea that Michael would kill himself especially in that house! Memories would soon kick in, but she knew it would take a long time to heal. She stood in the middle of the floor and wept. Her knees folded and she fell to the floor crying hysterically! Once she pulled herself together, she had to call all of her business contacts and friends to cancel their wedding plans. Maria never asks for much in life, and when she began dating Michael, and he proposed to her, she thought, *"I finally have someone that really loves me"*. But she had no idea that their relationship would end in tragedy.

One year went by since Michael's suicide death. Maria had repainted and refurnished the glass house. She had been seeing Kenny, Michael's friend the nightclub owner. Kenny had been taking good care of Maria since Michael's death. They had been dating exclusively. He knew she had breast cancer, but cared about her and wouldn't let anything keep him from her. Maria had fallen in love with Kenny; she never thought she could love again. But Kenny embraced her with all that he had; they had even talked about getting married. Kenny's family adored Maria and knew what a good woman she was. He didn't want to impose on her by moving in so he waited until after he'd proposed to her to move in.

One evening while watching a movie together, Kenny looked over at Maria on the sofa, held her hands tight and cleared his throat.

"Maria, I know we've only been dating a short time, but I have fallen in love with you. I can't give you all of what Michael gave you, but I can give you my heart, will you marry me?"

Maria paused, and thought, *"Most women in a life time get one proposal or none, and I got two!"* And she softly replied.

"Oh, yes, Kenny, I will marry you."

"Well, you've just made me the happiest man alive! Maria I plan to give you everything I possibly can, but more than anything I want to give you my heart."

"And that's all I need," Maria said.

He smiled, and hugged her as they locked lips gently on the sofa. Kenny didn't have a ring to give to Maria like Michael did, because he proposed unexpectedly. Michael had always had everything thought out and planned to a "T". Kenny didn't have quite the resources that Michael did, but he was caring and sincere.

Maria didn't feel like planning another wedding, but she did. Her sister, Adora helped her with the wedding plans, and she was proud that her sister had bounced back from the tragedy that she faced a year ago. Her mother was very supportive. Her mother had chosen her wedding colors as pink and white, and she chose to have an outside wedding this time, a small wedding just as before with sweet handsome Michael. Although, Maria was a millionaire by inheritance, she was the same ole down-to-earth girl that used to clean homes for a living. She didn't misuse any of the money that Michael left her in his Will.

Kenny never asks her for anything. He was the man and knew his role. So, he knew he had to provide for her. His nightclub had went down, but he kept it open hoping for business to pick up. With the economy the way it was, people were not spending their hard earned money on entertainment as much. So, Maria stepped up, and she helped Kenny with the Nightclub expenses.

Kenny stayed at the club less and less, because business was slow, and Maria's health was going down. Her sister and Mom thought she should put their wedding plans on hold, but Maria didn't want to postpone another wedding. So, she continued her wedding plans. Kenny was ecstatic that he would be married for the first time. Either of them had children, so he wanted a child with his soon-to-be wife, Maria.

Eventually, Kenny had to move in with his fiancé because the nightclub's overhead exceeded what he profited. While Maria was helping with his expenses, he felt bad because he was used to providing for himself. Kenny was more than a business owner, an independent man, and provider for his woman. He was just down on his luck and he had no idea what to do to survive, so he began to do cocaine, and drink a lot.

It was Friday night, and Kenny took Maria out to dance, drinks and have dinner afterwards. Maria had the time of her life with Kenny! She excused herself to go to the ladies room.

"I'll be right back Kenny."

"Okay" said Kenny, as he reached into his back pocket to grab something.

FOR LOVE OR MONEY?

A few minutes later, Maria came back to the table and laid her head on Kenny's shoulder.

"I'm ready to go honey," said Maria.

"Well, finish your drink first baby, and then we will jet outta here."

And Maria drank all of her drink and let out this loud burp, and they laughed.

"Oh, Kenny thank you for such a lovely night out honey."

"I hope you enjoyed it," said Kenny.

"I did, I really did."

As Kenny got up from the table; he reached out for Maria's hand. She staggered with a light buzz. He walked with confidence and she walked right beside him. The valet attendant grabbed Kenny's keys as they exited the building, and he drove the shiny black Cadillac Escalade around to the front of the restaurant. Kenny assisted Maria inside the Escalade, and closed her door. People admired them all night long, especially when they were on the dance floor. They were such a handsome couple.

Maria fell asleep on the way home. Her head drooped to the side; she was tired from making wedding plans all day, and dancing all night. Kenny just admired her while she was sleeping. He turned on some soft jazz on his satellite radio, and cruised home. Once they pulled into the driveway, he got out, and walked over to Maria's side of the Escalade, and picked her up and carried her into the house. He walked up the twenty flights of stairs, and placed her into the king size bed. He undressed her, and put her red silky nightgown on her. He then decided to take it off, and he made love to her all night.

The next morning, Kenny got up and showered, and he went down stairs to cook Maria breakfast. He cleaned up, and he even pre-pared Maria's clothes for the day. In his mind, he planned to spend the day with her. The hour was getting late; Kenny thought Maria should have been up by now. So, he went up to the bedroom to check on her, because Maria never came down for breakfast.

"Hey Maria, honey, breakfast is waiting for you," whispered Kenny.

No reply, so, Kenny walked closer to the bed and peeked underneath the thick covers, because Maria had always liked to sleep with the covers up over her head. She found comfort in that and it made the room darker. Still with no reply, so he peeled the covers back, and shook her, and she still wouldn't move.

"Maria honey, are you okay?"

And he kept shaking her and calling her name. "Maria, Maria, Maria."

Maria never answered; she passed away in her sleep. Her Cancer was in remission, and her body was healing from all of the chemotherapy. But Kenny already knew that's not what killed her. He had poisoned her drink at the club when she got up to go to the ladies room.

Kenny just slumped on the side of the bed onto the floor, and cried. He acted like he couldn't believe that Maria died. He pretended to be overwhelmed with grief, and sadness. He could just remember that he just made love to her thru the night, and how they had the best time ever out dancing, and drinking, with everyone watching and admiring their relationship. Now, he was faced with the death of the woman he was about to marry. The woman he pretended that he loved, but it was just for the money. Kenny was delirious, and couldn't accept that Maria just died because of him. So, he raised her limp body out of bed, and put her into the bathtub, running ice-cold water over her body, hoping she would wake up. He murmured, *"Apparently, she must have just died a few hours ago, because her body was still warm"*.

"Maria, wake up baby!"

FOR LOVE OR MONEY?

He had the nerves to have tears all over his face! He pulled her out of the bathtub, and dried her off, and then he put on the clothes that he had laid out for her. Kenny was beginning to be delusional. He put perfume and lipstick on her while he was talking to her as if she was alive. And then he brushed her hair. Kenny was about to lose his mind. He knew he committed Maria's murder by poisoning her drink the night before, yet he was in denial. He still hadn't called the police. In his mind, she wasn't dead, at least not by him. He didn't want them to find out that she had been poisoned. His alibi would be she died from cancer and then he could collect her insurance policy and other monies after they were married. After, he got Maria's deceased body dressed; he called the Bishop to set their wedding date for tomorrow.

"Hello" answered the Bishop.

Kenny explained what his call was for. "Yes, it's a last minute notice Bishop, but we are ready to do this."

"Okay, so we will do your nuptials tomorrow morning at 12 noon at the church," said the Bishop.

"Okay, thank you so much Bishop."

Kenny knew he wouldn't get anything from Maria's death, because they weren't married, but he was still hoping, trying to think of a way to benefit. Even though he thought he loved her, he didn't love her real like Michael did Patricia. So, he wanted to be married to Maria, and then when she died from cancer he could inherit all that Michael had left her in his Will. He had planned for them to go get a Will today, but it was too late. Kenny was no better than Patricia in a sense. He was greedy, and wanted everything for himself. Even though Maria was helping with the nightclub he owned, it wasn't enough for Kenny. He ultimately wanted it all. And he would go to any lengths to get it.

So, the next morning, Kenny woke up as if nothing was wrong. He never called the police, paramedics, Maria's family, or his family to tell them that Maria passed just yesterday. Kenny was in it to win it!

FOR LOVE OR MONEY?

He'd always envied the things that Michael had, even Patricia. He wanted the Maid, in more ways than one. He used to flirt with Maria, but she wouldn't respond because her heart was with Michael. That's the reason he told Michael when he saw Patricia at his club cheating with Yolanda. It wasn't because he had to "come correct" to Michael with evidence of her cheating. He wanted ultimately to destroy his marriage, and he and Yolanda had both planned to be together and live off of Michael's money that Yolanda was receiving from Patricia. Their years of devious planning backfired, and neither of them got anything.

Maria's body was already dressed from the day before. Kenny had put her into this elegant black and white dress and black Stilettos. She had on dark sunglasses, so that no one could see her eyes closed and pale face. He wrapped a leather arm bag around her shoulder, as if she were ready to go out on the town. When they first began dating, Kenny had secretly recorded her voice saying, *"I do"*. He would always ask her on the phone if she loved him, and she would say, *"Yes, I do Kenny"*. So, he could use this recorder if she never agreed to marry him, but he never thought he would really have to use it. Dead or alive, he was going to force Maria to marry him.

He was getting weirder by the minute. He went into the bathroom to shower, and shave. He began conversing with Maria as if she could answer him back.

"Hey babe, you like the dress you got on? I guess you do, you didn't say anything about it." And he laughed out loud with no sense of remorse.

Kenny got out of the shower, and dried off. He put on his black suit, white shirt, and shoes. He had gotten a regular ring out of Maria's jewelry box to place on her finger. Kenny was desperate for this inheritance, and he would go to any length to get it! His business was in foreclosure and he was behind on his Escalade payments, and he had promised Yolanda the world years ago. Bill collector's had been calling him for months, and Maria never knew it because Kenny knew how to keep everything on the down low. He was always the "cool" one. So, nobody ever knew when something was wrong in Kenny's life, or at the club.

Kenny started pacing the floor, because he couldn't figure out a way to get Maria's body out of the house so, he went out and bought a wheel chair. *"Here baby, I'll be right back"*, and he placed the remote control in Maria's hand, and then he kissed Maria's deceased body on the forehead.

He went to the Salvation Army to get a wheelchair for Maria's body. He purchased the first one he saw. The morning was getting late and he knew he had to be at the church at 12 noon to meet the Bishop. So, he purchased the wheelchair, and folded it up, and placed it in the back of his Escalade. Once he got home, he opened the back door to get the wheel chair out, and the neighbors saw him struggling to get it out, so he offered to help.

"Hey Sir, you need some help with that?"

"No, I think I have it."

"Okay, if you don't mind me asking, did Maria hurt herself?"

"No, she didn't, it's for my mom, and she's coming in from out of town today and has a hard time getting around."

"Oh, okay, well let me know if you need help with anything," the neighbor said.

"Okay, I appreciate it man, thanks!" said Kenny.

His head begun to bead up with sweat from all the questions his nosey neighbor was asking, Kenny just wished he'd get the hell away from him so he could leave.

Kenny finally got the wheelchair out of his vehicle, without any more distractions, and pushed it into the house. He walked ups-tairs, and picked up Maria's body, and placed her in his arms, walked slowly down the stairs, and put her body in the wheelchair. Maria's body was hardening, her skin was darkening and she was beginning to smell. Kenny's sick mind jokingly said *"Honey, I thought you took a bath this morning?"* and he burst out laughing, as he sat her body up in his Escalade to take her over to the church to wed her. After he placed her in her seat, he strapped her in, and put her wheelchair in the back, and drove off. He turned on his satellite radio as if they were enjoying an outing together. He even cracked Maria's window so she could get some air.

Once he arrived at the church, he saw the Bishops old 1974 blue Cadillac, with a busted windshield, and rusty hubcaps. But there was another car parked behind his. However, Kenny didn't know whom that car belonged too. He was willing to pay the Bishop one thousand dollars for a quick ceremony, so that he could inherit millions. But even if he pulled this off, how would he reserve Maria's body until he made a claim on her from dying of cancer? Kenny was a sick individual; all he could see was dollar signs especially because of the financial problems he had incurred. He knew his big payday was coming after all. He and Yolanda were born for each other.

Kenny parked his Escalade in the church's visitor's space. It was the closest to the door. He hopped out, sweaty and nervous, but playing it cool. He opened the back door to get the wheelchair, and then he reached for Maria's body, grabbed her and sat her in the chair. Her purse was wedged underneath her arm as if someone was going to steal it, and her sunglasses were on her face crooked. Kenny quickly straightened her glasses; he noticed her appearance and quickly pushed her inside the church. He had a lot of nerves, and he was very creepy. A woman from across the street observed him wheeling in this lady who appeared to be asleep, and real stiff, but she was drunk and uncertain. So, she got up, and stumbled to the pay phone and called the Police to report what she saw.

Yolanda had met Kenny up at the church. He knew she would be there, because she was all about money. Yolanda was always waiting for a handout, even if it was from the death of someone. Kenny seemed genuine towards everyone until he had a crisis, and then it was all about Kenny. He covered up his evil thoughts and behavior very well. However, they had this planned for quite some time.

The Police arrived at the church a few minutes later. Kenny looked shocked when they walked thru the door. The Officer entered into the church with his hand on his gun.

"Sir, we have a report that someone with suspicious activity was in the building, are you authorized to be in here?"

Kenny paused and took off running thru the wide double doors, and he cut past trees in the back of the church. He crossed the street without looking he was running so fast, he looked up, and a truck hit him and broke his legs. The driver of the vehicle crashed into a tree.

Yolanda stood there and said to the Officer" Yes sir, he was holding me hostage after he killed Maria, that lady" and she pointed to the wheelchair holding Maria's body.

The Officer called for backup immediately, and asks Yolanda if she was okay. He took a statement from Yolanda, and she acted as if she never knew whom Kenny was. The Officer called the Coroner to pick up Maria's body, and Yolanda was shaking from her lies as she was escorted out of the church and to her car.

The man that hit Kenny wasn't hurt, so he jumped out of his truck to see if Kenny was okay. Kenny begged him not to call the ambulance, because he didn't want to be arrested, but he couldn't move he was paralyzed from his waist down. Once the police arrived on the scene after chasing Kenny, they read him his rights, and then they allowed the ambulance to take him to the hospital to be treated.

Once Kenny was well enough to be released, he went directly to Prison for the murder of his fiancée Maria. He had months and months of physical therapy, but he never recovered from his injury that broke his leg and damaged his spine. Kenny was sentenced seventy-five years in prison, and he was never able to walk again. The men in prison used his body, and he turned homosexual after serving just five

years of his seventy-five. They would beat him up, because they knew
he wasn't able to defend himself. Take his money, and throw him
down in the cell on the bed, gag his mouth with a sock, and had anal
and oral sex with him because they knew he couldn't move. In the beginning he tried to fight back, but after other prisoners had busted out
all his teeth, concussions, broken arms, and bruises he finally gave up
the fight. He just allowed them to do whatever they wanted too to him,
which meant no more beatings.

After ten years in prison Kenny was diagnosed with HIV, it
was bad, and he just wanted his life to end. He was paralyzed, gay, and
dying from AIDS. Yolanda went to visit him a few times over the ten
years he had served, but all he heard from her was grief. He hated
when she came, but he knew nobody else would come. He was down
to one hundred pounds. Kenny used to be this handsome hunk-of-a-
man like Michael. They did body building together, educated, had successful businesses; they would get all the women, and then some. They
had everything any successful person could want. But in the end, because of their greediness, they lost everything, even their own lives!

Yolanda knew Kenny didn't have anyone, so she went to the
prison to see Kenny and to keep him humiliated. She called him an
"old gay bitch", even in his sickness. Yolanda just enjoyed seeing others way down on their luck. Kenny urinated in his pants, and his
wheelchair was always filthy and smelly. Everyone kept him isolated
from them, and nobody would help, not even Yolanda when she visited. He had feces in his chair, and Yolanda put on a glove as if she
was going to help him get cleaned up, and she would take the feces
and stick it in his mouth. A tear fell down Kenny's face when she did
that. All Kenny could do was cry. Yolanda got back at him from telling Michael about her love affair with Patricia years ago. He had
messed up her plans, and she was paying him back for all that he had
done to her. Even though Yolanda, and Kenny plotted this big scheme
that back-fired, Yolanda hated Kenny, and she told him she was glad
he was dying and that he deserved everything that happened to him.
As sickly as Kenny was, all he could do was sit there and listen. He
never ask the guards to not allow Yolanda to come back to visit because she was his only visitor. He had no more friends, and his family

disowned him, not because of AIDS, but because he was a murderer. But Yolanda was stupid enough to continue visiting him just to make him feel worse than he already did. She was a prime example of "misery loves company".

The guards would always watch Yolanda coming and going from the Prison. Her last visit she had an argument with this husky guard about staying too long. So, her next visit he watched her time even closer. When Yolanda left the Prison, he snatched her arm, and pulled her into the Laundry room. She tried to fight him off of her, but he was too big, even for aggressive Yolanda to handle. He pushed her into this small closet and pulled off her clothes and raped her. Yolanda couldn't see who grabbed her, but she tried to scream, but he held her mouth tightly with his hand, and his gun was in her side. He began to say, *"shut up or I'll kill you"*. And as soon as he spoke she recognized his voice. He pushed her down on the floor and sodomized and beat her up with his nightstick. After he finished, he straightened his clothes, and wiped off his sweaty face, and then he walked out as if nothing had happened. Yolanda lay on the floor unconscious in a pool of blood where the Officer had beaten her repeatedly with his nightstick. Her face was swollen, and she was naked. And no one knew she was there for days.

The Janitor found her a few days later unconscious. He called for help, and picked her up and took her to the infirmary for treatment. Kenny never knew why she didn't come by to see him for a few days; he thought she was just punishing him so he wouldn't have a visitor.

The Doctor ran several tests on Yolanda, and her family came to see her after they transferred her into another hospital. When Yolanda became conscious, the Doctor delivered some horrific news to her. He informed her that she was HIV positive. The guard that raped her was the man that had sex with Kenny and he had full blown AIDS, and he infected Yolanda just as he did many other helpless inmates. He had it out for Yolanda because Kenny told him to get her for him one day, and he did. Even in Kenny's sickness, he was still evil. He and Yolanda hated each other over all those years.

FOR LOVE OR MONEY?

"Oh, my God, I have what?" Yolanda said.

"We have run several tests (including a pregnancy test) and each one came back HIV positive, and you're pregnant." I'm sorry ma'am, but we can give you a good list of Physicians who can help treat you for this illness", and he touched her shoulder and turned and walked away.

Yolanda just sat up in her hospital bed, and thought about all the wrong she had done, and how she had ruined Patricia's life, marriage, and how she had her rapped that rainy night. She was definitely reaping what she had sown. She thought she was invincible. She cried and her family just walked out in disgust, because they had thought *why she was going to see Kenny in Prison anyway?* Yolanda just cried for hours, and she knew her life would never be the same. Even if she lived with HIV or a child, it would never be the same. Should she keep a child that she would never live to see, or know its father? Or should she terminate her pregnancy?

A few days went by and the Doctor released Yolanda from the hospital, but she had to call a cab to pick her up, because her own family disowned her. She went back to her apartment depressed, pregnant and she had contracted HIV from the Prison Guard that raped her. She wanted to pay the world back from her mistakes, so she posted her add online on a dating site, but she used old pictures of how she used to look. She fixed up her profile to look and sound nice. She sounded very successful, sincere and caring. Every day she would check her messages to see if she had any prospects. She had so many hits to her page so, she selected to chat with only the guys that looked attractive and who appeared like they had money.

She chatted for a few days and then she initiated meeting them one night. One guys name was Jason and the other was Ronald, both guys' profiles read that they were 36, single, eligible, no children, and seeking a serious relationship. So, Yolanda pursued them both, it was just a matter of "who would take her bait first".

It was a Friday night and Yolanda was feeling pretty good after she medicated herself, and she was drinking. So, she called up Jason, who was excited to meet her in a few hours at an R& B club for their first "meet and greet". She put on a spaghetti strap black silky dress, high heels, and put her hair up with long dangle earrings on. Jason was already at the club waiting for her in a booth. He watched the door for Yolanda to walk thru from the way she had described herself in the email. So, as soon as she walked thru the door, he knew who she was. Everybody was checking her out. Jason got up, and approached her.

"Well, hello, lovely lady you must be Yolanda?"

"Why yes", said Yolanda.

"And you must be Jason?"

"Yes, I am, come this way darling'" said Jason.

Yolanda already had a buzz from drinking before she left home, she smoked a joint too, plus she was on pain meds.

"So, how are you this evening?" Yolanda said.

"Oh, I'm doing much better now that you have arrived," said Jason.

"Did you find your way okay?" said Yolanda.

"Yes, I did."

"Do you come here often?" ask Yolanda.

"No, this is my first time here, but I get around pretty well."

"So, what's a good looking guy like you doing single?"

"I just haven't met the right person," said Jason. "But perhaps you could be that right person?"

"Hmmm, you never know do you?" said Yolanda.

FOR LOVE OR MONEY?

Yolanda hated men, yet she still found them attractive. She had been a lesbian all her life, but now she decided to date all the men she could since nothing else was going right for her.

The music was nice; and Teddy Pendergrass's song was playing *"Turn off the Lights"* it set the tone for whatever. The atmosphere was cozy, and they began to sit closer as the night progressed.

"Well, would you like to dance Miss Yolanda?"

"Yes, I'd like that."

They danced close all night; even after several drinks and dinner they were not ready to leave. The mood was still hot; everybody was dancing the night away! Jason didn't want to leave her either. His hands were all over her. They were attached like they'd known each other for a couple for years.

"Yolanda, I know we just met, but will you spend the night with me?"

"Are you sure you want to do that so soon?"

"Yes, I'm really feeling you baby. Let's get us a Hotel for the night."

Yolanda winked her eye at Jason, rubbed his arm, and sensually agreed, and they got a hotel out by the nightclub they were at. They entered the hotel room; and he backed Yolanda up onto the bed, kissing her aggressively, panting hard like a dog. And then they ripped each other's clothes off. Yolanda pretended that she wanted him to use a condom, but he didn't because she looked "clean" and she didn't stop him. They made love all over the room, and ended up on the floor.

The next morning Jason got up smiling, because Yolanda had left him a note on his bathroom towel. He showered, stepped out, and picked up his towel to dry off. He opened the note that Yolanda left him, and read it silent. He thought the note would say, *"What a great time she had with him last night and that she wanted to see him again. "* But, the note read *"Hey Jason, I had fun infecting you with the HIV virus last night!"* His mouth dropped wide open, and he said *"Oh, my God, what have I done, what will I tell my wife!"* Jason was married, yet he was online dating different women pretending to be single, now he had paid the ultimate price for sleeping around, married and especially unprotected.

Yolanda was home online seeking out her next victim; she made arrangements to see Ronald. She was hurt mentally, emotionally, physically and spiritually. She planned to bring down as many men as she possible could because she was raped, and infected with this deadly disease, and she knew she wouldn't ever have another real relationship with anyone, a man or a woman, because of her illness.

Yolanda was now eight weeks pregnant and still not showing. She wanted to have an abortion, but she was so distraught she didn't know what to do. But she knew she didn't want to see her child in a single parent home, in foster care and /or she didn't want her child to come into the world battling AIDS itself. She knew she would have to choose one way or the other very soon.

Yolanda logged onto the computer and she began to IM Ronald. And she typed in...

"Hi Ronald, how are you today?"

"I'm doing great, how are you sexy lady?" replied Ronald.

"I'm doing well, can't hardly wait to meet you though." said Yolanda.

"Well, that's nice to hear, I can't wait to meet you either."

"Let's say we meet tonight at The Three Dollar Café on Main Street say about 7 o'clock P.M? Yolanda suggested.

"Okay, that sounds great, I'll be there at 6:45," said Ronald.

"Wonderful, see you then love," said Ronald.

FOR LOVE OR MONEY?

So, Yolanda logged off her computer, and was getting ready for her date. They had exchanged phone numbers, and set up the place and time to meet. Yolanda lit up a joint, and pulled out her Red Rum. She started smoking and drinking shots, planning to damage another life. Yolanda looked in the mirror at herself and thought, *"With all this ass, I know he will want this"*. So, she put on a tight mini-skirt and sweet smelling perfume to entice Ronald, and she knew he would fall for her bait.

Yolanda pulled into the "Three Dollar Café", parked her car and before she could walk inside she saw Ronald walking towards the door, he looked just like his picture, medium height, dark and hand-some.

"Well, hello Ronald."

"Hi, you must be Yolanda?"

"Yes, in the flesh" said Yolanda. Twitching her eyes, and pushing out her chest so that Ronald would notice her breast.

"Wow, you look stunning!"

"Well, Thank you," said Yolanda. And he held the door open for her to walk thru.

"Two for dinner?" ask the Host.

"Yes", replied Ronald.

The Host escorted them to a seat, but Yolanda said "No, we will just sit at the bar." And she stumbled towards the bar.

"Oh, okay, no problem", said the Host.

"You aren't hungry" Ronald said.

"Nope, I just need a drink."

"Well, it seems to me that you've had enough to drink already." Ronald said.

"Well, for your information I haven't, now buy a gal a drink!"

Ronald didn't like loud women and especially drunken women, so he got up and left her sitting at the bar alone.

A few weeks went by, and Yolanda contacted Ronald again. She apologized several times about their first date. Ronald accepted her apology, and they agreed to meet again. This time they met for dinner at the Cheese Cake Factory. Afterwards Yolanda invited herself to his place, and he agreed. Ronald couldn't resist Yolanda's legs and thighs. She knew just what to wear. She knew what a black man loved, a big behind, and thick thighs, and she showed it all to him. She kissed all over him, and undressed him like it was their honeymoon. He reached for a condom from his wallet, but Yolanda convinced him it was okay to not use a condom, and that she hadn't had sex in over a year, and he believed her, just as she did Jason.

When Ronald woke up, he walked to his bathroom and turned on the water, looked down at his towel on the sink, and opened a note from Yolanda, and read it…. *"Welcome to the world of HIV asshole."* He sat on the toilet in disbelief, made a call to Yolanda but she didn't answer. He then went online to warn others to leave her alone. He reported her to the police, and to the dating agency online. He gave out her profile information to warn other men. Within an instant, several other men had been in contact sexually with Yolanda and she had infected them also. Yolanda was on a great mission to destroy as many people as she could. Since her life was a shamble, she wanted everyone else's to be too.

She had infected Doctors, Lawyers, Married men, and single men, anyone she could get revenge on because of what had happened to her. Yolanda was molested as a child, and grew to hate all men, that's how she became a lesbian. She despised them, and hated any man that tried

113

to be with her. She enjoyed destroying others' lives like Patricia's marriage, Kenny, Jason, Ronald, and others that came in contact with her. Since she was a child, with all that went on in her life, Yolanda was doomed to fail.

Yolanda turned on the TV and saw her picture on TV. Her family called her and asks her if she was crazy for spreading the HIV virus on purpose?

She replied, "I don't care about myself or anyone else, my life is over."

And then she hung up the phone. Anyone that saw the News knew to watch out for Yolanda, and knew that she was spreading HIV. However, her family had no idea that she was pregnant.

Nine months had passed by, and Yolanda gave birth to a beautiful and healthy baby boy. He did not contract the virus in the womb. But Yolanda's health was failing right after her little boy turned one year old, and the women whose husbands she had slept with contacted her by phone. Jason had spread the virus to his wife, and Ronald who was DL had spread it to his male partner, who was married to another woman as well.

Yolanda said, "Well it seems that everyone got what they deserved for cheating." And Jason's wife screamed thru the phone, turning red in the face.

"I hope you burn in Hell!" and then she just slammed the phone down in Yolanda's face.

Yolanda had started losing weight, and her baby boy Isaiah was now 3 years old, but she was getting ready to lose him to the state. She was physically abusing him. He was undernourished and underweight. So, the state took custody of him, and several months later she died from complications of full-blown AIDS. After everyone Yolanda had infected came forth, Jason and Ronald had become good friends, and some had even mended their relationships back with their wives, and significant others over time.

Yolanda's family gave her a sad home going, and they had adopted her son Isaiah, thinking that they would benefit from the state. It took two years to get him, but they finally got him. They had always hated Yolanda's life style and in many ways were glad she was gone.

Many years had passed by with so many lives destroyed in the process. Isaiah was now seventeen years old. He was tall, handsome, and very muscular and he grew up to learn about his mom. He couldn't believe that she had done all those things to hurt herself and others. Yolanda's family had turned him against his own mom by all the negative things they had told him. And they had mistreated him too over the past ten years. He was trailing in his mom's footsteps, and couldn't hold a job, and he drank and smoked a lot. Isaiah stayed out all times of day and night. Yolanda's mom had prostituted him for the past ten years, but he never told the adoption agency out of fear.

His own grandmother, very obese, wearing a nappy blond wig, with long blue acrylic nails told him that he would never amount to anything. And that he was a loser just like his mom, and that he never knew his dad because his mom was a whore. Isaiah was abused mentally, verbally and sexually. Any money that he made out on the street he had to give it to his grandmother to help pay her bills. And if there was anything left over, he could have what was left, which usually wouldn't be much.

Anything that Isaiah couldn't buy; he stole from others. To get money, he had slept with people of all ages, races, and genders, single or married. He had lost his own identity by sleeping with men and women. One of his clients was gay, but he didn't care, he just knew his grandmother would disown him if he didn't turn tricks and bring her home plenty of cash. He had become his Grandmother's sole provider. She reminded him everyday that he would be outside, homeless and helpless if she hadn't took him in.

115

FOR LOVE OR MONEY?

Isaiah had developed many regular clients, and one of them was Ronald. Ronald was the online DL, brother that had slept with Yolanda, Isaiah's mom. Ronald was much older than Isaiah, but either of them didn't care. Ronald was divorced for some years now. Once his wife found out that he was DL, and had contracted HIV, she couldn't take anymore of his deception, so she left. However, Ronald wasn't honest with Isaiah. He never told him he was DL, HIV positive or that he contracted HIV from his mom.

One day they had this heart to heart talk, because similar names and situations kept coming up. Isaiah had told Ronald about his mom, and how his grandmother treated him all those years. Ronald felt horrible, and he offered for Isaiah to live with him, but he was afraid to. He didn't want to leave his grandmother because he was brain washed into thinking that no one else would love him or take care of him the way that she did. Even though he had one more year before he turned eighteen, she had always threatened to send him back to the state. And he hated living there.

"Isaiah, I have something to tell you."

"What is it? Are you cheating on me?" ask Isaiah.

"No, that's not it," said Ronald.

"Well, you're killing me with the suspense, just tell me."

"I used to know your mom."

"What? How? Isaiah said.

"Oh shit, are you my dad?"

Ronald laughed, "No, I'm not your dad."

"I met your mom online years ago and we used to sleep with each other."

FOR LOVE OR MONEY?

"So, tell me you don't have HIV?"

"Yeah, I do"…Ronald replied and he backed away from Isaiah.

"And you've been sleeping with me unprotected?"

"I'm sorry Isaiah."

"I thought you cared about me, grandma was right? She said nobody else cared about me, and she was right."

Isaiah reached over and slapped Ronald in his face, and ran out of the room. Ronald never meant to hurt Isaiah, but he also never meant to fall in love with him either.

Isaiah went a few days later to be tested, and his results came back negative. He was so grateful that he wasn't infected. He lived this promiscuous teen lifestyle, and he was blessed to not have been infected. He never spoke to Ronald again.

At the tender age of twenty-one, Isaiah took inventory on himself, and began to take responsibility for his own life. He began to turn his life around with prayer and going back to school. He didn't want to become his mother, or prove his grandma to be right. He went to college, it was hard financially, but he earned his Master's degree after many years with hard work and dedication. He became a Radio Host at 30, and later held his own radio talk show

"Isaiah's Hour" was the name of his show. It was from 2-3pm Monday thru Friday. He had cleaned up his image, and was no longer confused about his sexuality. He had gotten his own five bedroom home, own car, and lost contact with his grandmother who abused him mentally, sexually and emotionally for so many years. All he had been thru just made him a stronger man.

At the end of a workweek, the topic was open for callers to call in to Isaiah's Show to discuss whatever was on their mind. It was called

FOR LOVE OR MONEY?

"free topic Friday". The phones were ringing off the hook, and Isaiah was pleased that his ratings were thru the roof!

"Yes, caller, what's on your mind today?" Isaiah answered.

Calls were coming in from people everywhere who were black, white, gay, straight, DL, bi-sexual, involved, married, and single.

"Ahhh, yes, Hi Isaiah" ..."I am a married DL male and I've been married for ten years, and my wife has no idea that I enjoy being with men. I lie to her to get out of the house, but it's easy, because she trust me. So, I'm out all the time doing my thing. But my question is should I tell her, and move on? Or go ahead and practice the phrase "what you don't know won't hurt you?" said the caller.

The next caller called in and said, "I am a single bi-sexual female, and I'm engaged to be married to my high school sweetheart, should I still get married?

The next caller said "I am a straight female and suspected that my boyfriend was cheating on me with another woman, but I found out thru a mutual friend that it's true, but it was with a man, I confronted him and he said would it matter if it were a woman?"

The last caller before a commercial called and said "I just found out that my husband of twenty years has HIV, I was tested and I was negative, should I leave him?"

Isaiah was overwhelmed with all the calls that came thru to his radio show, but he was proud that he had accomplished his education and career goal at age thirty and that he finally realized he wasn't the only one who went thru something so damaging. The lines were lit up all across the phone.

"Okay, I will take my last caller for "free topic" Friday. Hello caller you are on the air?" ask Isaiah.

"Hi there, Isaiah how are you this morning?" ask the caller.

FOR LOVE OR MONEY?

"I'm good who is this?" said Isaiah.

"This is an old friend of yours when you were living with your grand-mother."

Isaiah paused, and took a deep breath. He knew he had a shabby past, and wondered who had come back to haunt him.

"Okay", and in his powerful radio toned voice, Isaiah said, "Who is this old friend?"
There was a long pause on the airwaves, and then the caller said, "This is Ronald."

Isaiah jumped out of his leather black high back chair in the studio, and said, "We have to take a commercial break."

Isaiah cut the call on the air, and ran out of the studio. He ask his staff to cover for him when they go back "live" in case he didn't make it back in time to finish today's show. Isaiah took the call on another phone.

Isaiah snatched the phone off the hook, breathing hard and answered excitedly!

"Hi Ronald, how are you, it's been a long time man?"

"Yeah, it has been, CONGRATULATIONS on your new show!"

"Oh, thank you man. What's up with you now?" said Isaiah.

"Well, I've been feeling pretty good, I actually feel healthier than ever!"

"So why did you come back here looking for me?" Isaiah said.

"Well, I heard your show a few months ago, and I just wanted to see you and congratulate you."

FOR LOVE OR MONEY?

Isaiah took a long pause and said, "Hmm, maybe we can meet up somewhere?"

After a long phone conversation, they both decided to meet not far from the radio station. Once they arrived at their meeting place, they both greeted each other with a handshake and hug.

"You're looking good Ronald, where you staying at now?"

"Right now I don't have a place; I'm crashing at a friend's place. My house went into foreclosure a couple of months ago," said Ronald.

"I'm sorry to hear that, but if you need to, you can stay with me for a little while."

"Really?" said Ronald.

"Yes, I have a five bedroom home, and there's plenty of space for you. Here are the directions, and a key lets go out for dinner and talk tonight, it's on me" said Isaiah.

"Okay, if you insist," Ronald said.

Even thru Ronald's dishonesty, Isaiah was very forgiving. He knew when he was down on his luck he needed someone too, and he thought we all need to be forgiven of something.

Isaiah put his head in his hand, and thought, *"what did I just do?"* He still had feelings for Ronald from back in the day. But he thought he was over the *"attraction-to-men"* thing. Isaiah went home and freshened up. Ronald wasn't in. But, Isaiah had planned a reservation dinner for them at a five star restaurant, valet parking, expensive cover charge for two, live Jazz band and two free tickets to the next event where the band would be playing.

The time was getting late, and Isaiah had left the station early that day to prepare for the dinner date. He was impatiently pacing the floor nervously, biting his nails, after he'd gotten dressed and then Ronald finally showed up with a red rose for Isaiah, which meant, *"I love you"*. Isaiah calmed down when he heard Ronald come thru the door, rattling keys, and was even more surprised when he saw Ronald give him a red rose! He thought he had not overcome his feelings and the betrayal of Ronald, but found himself to be forgiving. Was it *fate or fatal* that they were reunited again?

"Hey you?" said Ronald, as he put down his unlocked briefcase, and handed Isaiah the rose with a very intimate hug.

"Hey, thanks for the rose. "I was getting worried about you, because it's getting late and I have a reservation set up for us at 9:30," said Isaiah.

"Well, that's fine, let me go freshen up then, and I'll be right down," said Ronald.

Ronald ran up the stairs, took a quick shower. But while Ronald was in the shower, Isaiah was curious about what he was carrying around, and he went thru his briefcase. He'd remembered the betrayal, but forgave, yet still felt the need to know what he was up to. He couldn't find anything, just some tax forms, old check stubs, credit card purchases, and gas receipts. So, he put everything back quickly as he heard Ronald come down the stairs. Ronald was pacing himself slowly walking down the stairs with one boot in front of the other, softly touching each step; he didn't want to appear too anxious. On the last step, he exhaled and said…

"Alright, are you ready?" Ronald asks.

"Yes, I'm ready," Isaiah said.

"Okay, then lets go paint the town!" said Ronald.

They both stepped out in studded jeans and white shirts, black blazer with pointed-toe black leather cowboy boots looking as sharp as ever! If all the women didn't notice them the men were sure too! They were dressed to kill and had a look to die for that would surely turn heads!

As they stepped out of Isaiah's two-seated dark Gray Maserati, everyone was looking. They knew they looked good and would turn heads all night long. The Valet attendant walked up to Isaiah's car and opened the door. Isaiah stepped out, and gave the attendant his keys to valet park his Maserati. The doorman greeted them with a smile, nodded his head, and opened the huge wooden stain glass door for Isaiah and Ronald to enter into the five-star restaurant. They looked around, especially Ronald; their table was already reserved, so they were escorted to their table near a huge bay window upstairs, overlooking a deep blue waterfall surrounded by tall healthy green plants. A pianist was playing, and the atmosphere had a tropical look and feel.

"There you are gentleman. Can I get you anything to drink?" said the Waiter.

They ordered their drinks and then read over the menu.

"Okay, gentleman, I'll be right back."

After the Waiter walked away, Ronald said, "May I ask you something?"

"Yeah, sure man, what's up?" …

"So, why did you forgive me and invite me into your home?"

There was a long pause, and Ronald thought he'd spoiled the evening with questions about the past.

"Hmmm, well, I think it's only right to forgive someone so that I can be free. And I ask you to stay with me because I know firsthand how it feels to be without somewhere to go."

"Well, thank you man" Ronald Said, and the Waiter brought their drinks to the table.

FOR LOVE OR MONEY?

"Are you men ready to order now?" said the Waiter.

So, they both placed their orders and begin to laugh and talk while listening to the enchanting mellow music. They looked into each other's eyes, with a glow that could stop the show.

After dinner, they went downstairs to listen to the Jazz band play. They sat at the bar and ordered more drinks. The band played many hits, and the house was packed! Ronald and Isaiah stood close together, and chatted all night, they closed the Jazz bar down. Ronald was getting a bit touchy. Isaiah liked it but he wasn't too big on public affection. After all, he thought he was over his attraction for men.

The night was over, and they drove home drunk. Thank God Isaiah didn't get a ticket. It would have been spread all over the news with him being a popular Radio Hosts. But for some reason he didn't care or wasn't thinking clearly that night to drink and get into his vehicle under the influence. Scrutiny was all around him, plus he was hiding his gay lifestyle from his friends and co-workers.

Once they made it home safe, Isaiah was too drunk to get his car parked into the garage, so he parked it crooked in the driveway, and stumbled to the other side of the car to get Ronald out. Neighbors were peeking out the window, because they heard him drive up at 4a.m with his windows down, and music bumping loud. Isaiah noticed that they were peeking and held up his middle finger and shouted...

"What the hell you lookin' at assholes?" And they quickly closed the curtains.

As they stumbled into the house, Ronald woke up just enough to realize they were home. Isaiah dumped Ronald on the sofa, and he began taking off Ronald's shirt. He unbuttoned his jeans and pulled off his boots so that he could just slide him out of his jeans. Isaiah began kissing all over Ronald, rubbing his chest, and giving him oral intimacy. Ronald just moaned. He was too drunk to move. But he enjoyed it.

When Isaiah was finished, he put the covers over Ronald and left him on the sofa and he went upstairs to bed.

Soon it would be bright morning, and the beginning of another day. Isaiah had been dating a sista name LaShawn off and on. She had no idea he'd ever liked being with men and she didn't know too much about his past. LaShawn called Isaiah at 9:00a.m. Ring Ring…Isaiah snatched the phone off the hook, and answered the phone in a weak voice.

"Hello" answered Isaiah.

"Hey what's up, you still asleep?" (In a loud voice) said LaShawn.

"Yes, I am."

"You sound terrible" said LaShawn.

"Well, LaShawn, I had a long night, we took some potential marketing clients out last night and I got in pretty late."

"Well, you invited me out to breakfast at 9:00am this morning, you don't remember?"

"Unfortunately, we won't make it today, we will have to go another time, okay" said Isaiah.

"You are so full of shit!" said LaShawn.

"Whatever" said Isaiah? And he hung up the phone.

LaShawn was a pushy drama queen and hated taking *"no"* for an answer. *"I'll fix his ass,"* she thought. So, she got into her car and drove to Isaiah's house uninvited.

Ronald finally woke up, with a hangover, but he managed to wobble up the stairs to his bedroom. Isaiah was coming from the restroom and heard Ronald's footsteps and peeked out his bedroom door.

FOR LOVE OR MONEY?

"Hey you, how are you feeling this morning?"

"Awe man my head is hurting bad" said Ronald.

"Well, step in here; (as he motioned with his hand for Ronald to come inside his room).

"I'll make you feel better Ron."

So, Ronald smiled, and went into Isaiah's bedroom, and they closed the door, and made love to each other again. It was the weekend so; Isaiah was off from work and wanted to spend all day with Ronald.

Isaiah tried hard to fight his feelings for Ronald, but Ronald was the first man that really ever truly loved him. Isaiah was from such brokenness and abuse that he was just glad to be accepted and loved by someone. And that "someone" was another man, Ronald. After they had made love, they fell asleep with their bodies close to one another.

LaShawn had arrived uninvited, because Isaiah had promised her a breakfast date, but he forgot, and cancelled at the last second. So she went to his house, parked her car around the backside of his street and walked to his house. Once she walked up, she saw his Maserati parked crooked in his driveway alongside of Ronald's car. She knew that he kept an extra house key under his doormat off in a hole in the concrete in case of an emergency. So, she took it out, opened the door and walked in quietly on her tiptoes.

She thought she'd find another woman in there, because she saw another car in his driveway. But to her surprise she saw a man's clothes on the sofa, but she assumed they were Isaiah's. She looked around for a woman's clothes, shoes, earrings, purse, etc. But she didn't see anything feminine lying around, that made her feel somewhat at ease. But she just felt something was wrong, so, she proceeded to the kitchen to get a knife just in case. LaShawn took her shoes off, and she walked upstairs quietly, hoping to get into bed with Isaiah.

FOR LOVE OR MONEY?

When she gently pushed the door open, she saw Isaiah lying in bed naked with another man!

Isaiah had never given LaShawn any inclination that he was DL or gay.

She screamed! "Oh, My God!!!" shouted LaShawn.

"What is this Isaiah?"

Isaiah opened his eyes and saw LaShawn standing over him with a butcher knife.

"What the hell are you doing here girl?" and he jumped out of bed naked!

"Well, I was coming to surprise you, and you're screwing a man!"

"LaShawn how in the hell did you get in my house?"

"Oh my God, that doesn't matter why didn't you tell me you liked men? You've been sleeping with me unprotected off and on for months Isaiah, LaShawn cried.

"Oh my God you bastard!" shaking the butcher knife at him profusely.

By now, Ronald jumped up, and grabbed Isaiah's house-robe from the foot of the bed, covering himself and embarrassed. Yet wondering whom this deranged woman was ranting and raving standing in the middle of the floor with a butcher knife! Isaiah ran towards LaShawn and grabbed the butcher knife out of her hand, and she fell to the floor pissed off and devastated that she'd been betrayed by Isaiah. The knife flew under the bed, and Ronald grabbed it just standing there waiting for something more to go down.

LaShawn asks "How could you do this to me Isaiah?"

FOR LOVE OR MONEY?

"I've been trying to tell you, but every time you come over you're so aggressive, that I never get a chance to say anything."

"Yes, I'll bet, but your thang gets hard when I get aggressive too don't it? And you never stopped me."

"Well, now you know that I am DL."

"DL my ass, you're gay Isaiah."

"What's wrong with you Isaiah? After all I've done for you and with you when nobody else was there?" LaShawn said.

"I'm sorry" Isaiah said.

"Yeah, you're sorry alright, you're sorry and you're tired!!" He grabbed her by the arm.

"Boy get your damn hands off me!"

LaShawn snatched her arm away from Isaiah and walked out of the room. She went downstairs, walked out, and slammed his door. He just stood in the middle of the bedroom floor looking confused.

Ronald asks "Hey Isaiah man, who was that? What was all that about?"

"LaShawn is a friend that I'd been seeing off and on for a while trying to find my sexuality, and get over you Ronald."
"Now, I've hurt her. And she was good to me."

"Yeah man but you gotta tell her I'm HIV positive and she needs to go get tested."

"Did you sleep with her unprotected Isaiah?"

"Yeah man, I did." said Isaiah.

FOR LOVE OR MONEY?

"So, you're no better than I Am," said Ronald.

Isaiah just held his head down in embarrassment of himself. He thought all the drama was over since he'd gotten away from his grandmother's abuse, prostitution, and he'd left behind his gay life-style and had a successful radio show.

Ronald went to the bathroom to shower, and Isaiah just sat at the foot of the bed wondering how he could have hurt LaShawn, knowing how devastated he was when Ronald betrayed him the same way. The house was silent after LaShawn came and stirred things up a bit. Now Ronald felt the same hurt and betrayal that he gave Isaiah.

Ronald packed his few things and left when he realized that Isaiah liked women too. He despised women, and wanted nothing to do with them. He thought women were only good for making babies. And that he could do anything women could sexually, but better. So, he went back to stay at his friends house. Ronald was so pissed off and hurt that he spread Isaiah's entire business in the streets. He even went to the Radio Station's President and Executive Producers of his show and told them whom Isaiah really was. Even though he had no right to destroy his career, he desperately tried to. But the Executive Producers waited for Isaiah to come clean, because after all he was bringing in the ratings.

Weeks and weeks went by, and Isaiah's show was still boom-ing with calls. Every line was lit up, and his show's ratings were thru the roof. Isaiah was ready and willing to answer all callers' question and take comments from callers.

"Hello, caller #1, what's your question or comment?"

"Hi Isaiah, I'd like to know if I was molested when I was little, should I forgive the abuser?"

Isaiah just shook his head in disgust that someone else was abused as a child, just as he was. He felt like the world was on his shoulders trying to help his callers.

FOR LOVE OR MONEY?

Several other callers called in that day, and Isaiah was just famished from no breaks that day, so he finally took his last call and gathered his things and left the station.

As soon as he got downstairs he found his car vandalized, and he called the police. He didn't want to wait for a cab, so he called LaShawn to come pick him up. They had some unfinished business to discuss. LaShawn came to pick up Isaiah and they went to his house. LaShawn told Isaiah that she was pregnant by him. And Isaiah was actually happy because he had no idea that he would have someone to call his own.

He hugged LaShawn and kissed her on the cheek. "So, what are we going to do?" LaShawn ask.

"Well, I hope you want this baby, because I do," said Isaiah.

"But, what about you sleeping with men? That's just unacceptable Isaiah."

"Listen, I know I've hurt you, and I've tried to be straight and kick this DL thing, but I guess I never got over Ronald."

"Well, do you want to be with him or me? I need to know now!" said LaShawn.

LaShawn really cared for and loved Isaiah but she was confused at Isaiah. She was the only one that's ever loved Isaiah.

"Look, there's a lot you need to know about me if we are going to be together. My mom died of AIDS, and my grandmother raised me in an abusive home. She abused me mentally, emotionally, physically, and sexually. She pimp me out for money, food or anything that she was too lazy to go out and get for herself."

"Uhhhuh" she murmured.

129

FOR LOVE OR MONEY?

LaShawn, I was turning tricks at a real young age. I was beaten, on drugs, and drinking, but I did what I had to do to survive on the streets. LaShawn, I had no place to go, no real family, and no one seemed to have cared of my well being as an innocent child. My own blood grandmother, who was supposed to be my primary caregiver and protector, she didn't love me and the Foster care system just didn't care, that's how I became so promiscuous. I've slept with men, women, black, white, Asian, Hispanics, married, gay, straight to make ends meet and to be accepted and win my grandmother's love. But nothing I did was ever good enough for her."

"Wow!" she replied.

"LaShawn, she only took me in to get money from the state which wasn't much. I think that my grandmother tried to punish me for what my mom did. Now that I've shared with you my most intimate part of my life, either you accept me, or you don't. I am sorry, that I didn't tell you sooner." And a tear fell from his eye.

LaShawn just sighed, and she said...

"I've been tested for HIV, and I was negative, thank God. And I am sorry that you went thru all of that as a child. How devastating that must have been for you?"
"Yes, it was, but I was so wrong for being intimate with you knowing that I had been with other men, and Ronald was infected with HIV, but he never transmitted it to me."

"So, do you want me or him?" asks LaShawn.

"I want to be with you, if you'll still have me?" said Isaiah.

"Yes, I'd like that Isaiah," said LaShawn.

"And now, I can finally have a real family" said Isaiah.

LaShawn carried out her pregnancy full term, but Isaiah had lost his job at the Radio Station, Ronald exposed him. His past indeed had come back to haunt him. Ronald was stalking him, and he hated that he had gone back to LaShawn. Ronald had always wanted to be with Isaiah. But he knew he no longer wanted to be in that lifestyle.

LaShawn had gone into labor, and Isaiah was nowhere to be found. He was with Ronald trying to get him to calm down. He thought if he talked to him, he would leave him alone. Isaiah had gone thru tumultuous times with LaShawn and Ronald, torn between two lovers; he just didn't know what to do anymore. He was trying to live right and make a family with LaShawn, wanting to regain some of what he lost as a boy. But he was still tempted by Ronald to please his flesh.

LaShawn had called for a cab to take her to the hospital nearby. She had no idea where Isaiah was. She was in labor for hours, and finally gave birth to a healthy baby boy. She named him Shawn, the suffix of her own first name, but she put Isaiah's name on his birth certificate as the father. She was exhausted from pushing, and screaming her throat was dry, and her face and hands were sweaty. The nurse patted her face dry, and gave her more ice chips. The baby was taken to be cleaned up, and for observation while LaShawn got some rest.

Several hours passed by and LaShawn had awakened, lying on her back looking up at the ceiling wondering where Isaiah could be. So, she reached for her cell phone next to the bed, and called him but no answer. So, she left him a message so he would know that he has a new baby boy, and what hospital they were in. She never sounded pissed off over the phone, because she wanted to be sure he'd come. She knew if she made him angry, he wouldn't come by. LaShawn wanted so much to have a family, and she saw other women with their husbands at their bedside after giving birth. Yet she sits all alone.

Isaiah met Ronald at a nearby café to see what he wanted, why he was following him when he knew he was exclusively dating LaShawn now.

"Isaiah, how can you do this to me man?"

FOR LOVE OR MONEY?

"Look, I had fun with you Ronald, but I've always wanted a real family, and LaShawn is carrying my baby man. I'm just trying to do right."

"Well, can LaShawn give you this?" Pointing at his pant, Ronald had a hard on.

Isaiah blushed a bit trying to fight the flesh and then he touched Ronald on the knee (Realizing that he was still caught up in a gay lifestyle, trying to be straight).

"So, what's it gonna be man?" ask Ronald.

Isaiah paused, and then he heard a beep on his cell phone, looking down at it, and then he noticed a missed call from LaShawn, but he never checked her voice message. Isaiah's old ways had quickly returned, and all he thought about was pleasing himself. After all, his grandmother turned him out as a child. However, he wanted to be with LaShawn to show the world that he was straight, and he knew he would have a stable family. But deep down his flesh and mind wanted to be with Ronald. Ronald just always made him feel accepted no matter what he had, was or had been through. He thought, *"How I would tell LaShawn that I can't be with her."* He had no idea that she had just given birth to his son while he was out trying to decide whom he wanted to sleep with or be with.

People were watching, especially women, because they were both handsome, athletic men, and always dressed sharp. Ronald didn't care; he took Isaiah by the hand, and led him to Isaiah's car. He leaned him up against the car, gave him a big strong hug and kissed him and told him that *"you my man for life"*. Isaiah just smiled at Ronald, gently pushing his hand away because they were in public, and they both got into Isaiah's car. This man that LaShawn use to date saw them huddled up together, and carrying on, he'd remember seeing him around LaShawn before. The women that were watching laughed at them; they thought *"what a waste of two good looking men"* with the shortage of men. Shook their heads in disgust and walked off.

132

FOR LOVE OR MONEY?

Ronald still lived with a friend, so they went to Isaiah's place. Ronald left his car in the parking lot, and he rode with Isaiah. Even though Isaiah had lost his job, he still had enough money saved up to survive on for a while longer, hoping that a bigger door would soon open. Isaiah was just the forgiving type. He didn't care who hurt him or what they did to him or even the motive behind what they did; he just wanted to be loved unconditionally. As they were riding down the street, Ronald starred at Isaiah, and he told him he loved him. Isaiah looked over at Ronald, and said *"I love you too man"*, either one not realizing the devastation that their relationship will cause on LaShawn and Isaiah's new-born baby.

LaShawn waited two days for Isaiah to call her at the hospital, but he never did. He had spent the last two days with Ronald. LaShawn knew something was wrong, because it wasn't like Isaiah to not call at all, she just didn't know what. LaShawn's nurse brought baby Shawn in to be diaper changed, breast fed, and then the baby fell asleep. The phone rang finally, and LaShawn thought it was Isaiah, but it was an old boyfriend, Fred, who used to date LaShawn.

"How did you get this number?" he giggled as if he could always keep up with her.

"I called your mom's house, and she told me that you'd be released at the Hospital today from having some nigga's baby."

"So, what jerk took my place?" Fred asks.

"Look Fred, I really don't feel good, and I don't feel like feuding with you, what do you want?"

"Well, being that yo supposed to be baby-daddy is out with some other fag, I have to come pick you up today don't I?" said Fred.

"What do you mean out with some other fag?"

"Look LaShawn, you know I've always been straight-up with you, and even though I cheated, I still love you, and want to be with you. But yo boy is gay, and he's cheating on you with another man. At least I was with a woman and not a man!"

"Well Fred cheating is cheating; does being with some other heifer make it better?"

"Nope, but I aint doing no fag either and spreading that shit."

"Whatever Fred, just come get me and lil man."

"Aiight, just tell me which hospital and I'll be on my way?"

Once Fred arrived at the hospital, he had to wait in the waiting area since he wasn't family. LaShawn had gotten all her and lil man's things packed and ready to go home. The hospital had given LaShawn a car seat for the baby because she had arrived in a cab, and didn't have one. Fred saw them come thru the lobby area, and quickly grabbed the baby carriage. He packed their things in his car, and the nurse helped LaShawn get into the car and wished them well.

A few weeks went by, and LaShawn still had not heard from Isaiah. He was afraid to call to tell her that he decided that he didn't want to be with her anymore, and he considered himself fully gay. LaShawn was hurt, but even though Fred was a cheater, and a loud mouth thug, he stepped up to the plate to help LaShawn with the baby.

Fred was a low-life drug dealer who used profanity most of the time, he was all tattooed down, gold teeth, with his pants dragging the ground, but he wouldn't let LaShawn and the baby need for anything. He brought the baby whatever he needed and gave LaShawn a few hundred dollars every week. LaShawn had a lot of pride, but she put her pride to the side because she needed his help. Isaiah had backed out on her, and had no idea that she had given birth weeks ago to his own flesh and blood. LaShawn thought Isaiah would be there for lil man, because of the abandonment he faced as a child. But, it was unfortunate that he chose his lover over his own child. She couldn't stand Fred, but she desperately needed his help.

FOR LOVE OR MONEY?

LaShawn had taken a nap, and the baby was asleep beside her. Fred was still there just chillin on the couch drinking alcohol, and smoking marijuana, and he heard LaShawn's cell phone buzz on the kitchen table, so he got up to answer it.

"Yo who dis?" ask Fred. There was a long pause at the other end of the phone.

"Ah, hello, may I speak with LaShawn please?"

Fred said, "Is this that fag that she had my baby with?"

"Look I don't know who you are punk, but you need to put LaShawn on the damn phone."

"Look here bro, why don't you stop calling her, she's not for you," said Fred.

LaShawn jumped up off the couch, and ran to snatch the phone from Fred. "What are you doing boy? Give me my damn phone! And she slapped Fred across the head.

"Hello, is this Isaiah?"

"Yes, it's me."

"Who was that answered your phone?"

"That's just a friend."

Fred yelled, "Just a friend?

"Yeah I'm the damn friend that's been helping you take care of this damn baby and throwing you money and shit errrr week!"

"LaShawn you had our baby?"

"Yes, Isaiah, I did."

"So, what happened to you, what's going on with you Isaiah?"

"LaShawn we need to talk."

"No, I think you've made your decision, go ahead and do what you do Isaiah, I just thought you changed."

"I'm sorry, I'll help you with the baby, I promise, but I'm in love with Ronald."

By the time LaShawn got off the phone in tears, Fred had left. He stormed out of the house. Even though he was tough, and all thugged out, he was tired of doing all the work and feeling unappreciated. Now that LaShawn had ran off Fred, and Isaiah broke up with her in a cowards way (over the phone) she had no one to help raise lil man. She was so hurt after what Isaiah had taken her through, and she cried for many months.

Seventeen years went by and LaShawn hated Isaiah all those years for allowing her to be in labor alone, choosing to be with a man over her, and walking out on their new son. She knew he had become a product of his past environment, but that was no excuse. LaShawn had become angry, and abusive to lil Shawn. She hated that he was a part of Isaiah, which made her abuse him as a child. She sold him for sex to older men and women just as Isaiah's grandmother did him. She instilled so much fear in him so that he wouldn't tell anyone. When lil Shawn was five, he was at the park and asks his mom to catch him when he jumped out of the swing, she said *"okay"*, but when he jumped she moved so that he would hit the ground. She would lock him up for hours if the house wasn't cleaned to her expectation. If she didn't have a good day at work, she would come home and beat him until his skin bled. She made him go to bed many nights hungry, and he would miss many days of school because he was ill. Once when he was ten years old, he didn't flush the toilet, she made him eat his own feces, and smashed the remains in his face. He was so afraid of her that he would urinate in the bed in fear of getting up to use the bathroom.

136

So, the next morning his mom would notice he urinated in the bed, and made him get a cup, and drink his own urine.

LaShawn had grown into this evil monster that she couldn't stand when she heard of such person thru Isaiah's life. But she punished lil Shawn because of who his father was and how he abandoned her. Her old boyfriend, Fred never came back, he wasn't about to put up with LaShawn's bullshit, but she saw him cruisin' the streets from time to time in his beat up lime green Chevrolet, with a cracked windshield sittin' on 22 inch chromed out rims, armor-all-down with no place to go.

Isaiah had lost Ronald to AIDS, but he never contracted it. Lil Shawn was twenty years old now, still living at home with his momma, prostituting, just as his daddy did. Isaiah never saw his son, so he had no idea that he had grown into what he was, selfish, and no good. Isaiah was depressed because Ronald died, and he never met anyone else like him. But he had some joy and pride in owning his own small company, which was a big step down from the popular radio-hosting gig he had.

Isaiah was riding around one night after closing the store, and he saw a handsome young gentleman on the corner. Isaiah just couldn't shake men, after all he did confess to being fully gay. He picked up the good looking twenty something year old man, and took him back to his place.

After he'd made love to him, they talked for hours, and he realized it was his own son he had just been intimate with! Isaiah slid out of bed in disgust, walked into his closet, pulled out a black shoebox, got his gun, and shot himself in the temple.

After the funeral, Lil Shawn left his mom, with no regrets, but he still loved her. He stopped prostituting, got his own place, slowly got his life together, found his own wife and family, and vowed to never touch another man again. He loved his wife, and took great care of his children. He hated that his mom abused him as a child, and later found out that his dad was treated the same way. He inherited everything that

Isaiah had, and everything that others were fighting over all those years, even before he was born. He had become a popular radio host just as his *dad* Isaiah had before Ronald destroyed his life. He quickly learned about greed, and that most people marry for all the wrong reasons, but he knew that his wife married him for love.

After many years went by, he researched his own family history; because his father's untimely death puzzled him. He never told anyone he slept with his own father one night while still in the life of prostitution, not even his wife. He found out about Michael, and Patricia, and how she'd been a lesbian with her best friend Yolanda, and how Patricia married Michael for his money. He'd found out about all the family abuse, greed over money, and misuse of family and friendships. He'd found out about so many things he was not proud of, but he knew why he did the things he'd done by being forced into prostitution, and having a hateful and uncaring gay parent, surrounded by greed in all their unstable ways. But he knew somehow it wasn't right, and he had a choice. And Shawn realized that their greed passed down from generations. Although he had been through an abusive childhood, he reaped the benefits from his and his families long suffering. Someone had to break the cycle, and it was Shawn. When he found the right woman that he knew cherished him for who he was, and not what he could give her, he married her. And she married him for unconditional love!

Shawn's wife was the ideal woman for him. She never put him down, or made him feel less of a man. She was a bright school teacher, and loved children. She worked in their community alongside her own children, trying to show them how to care for others and their community. They'd gone on mission trips and visited the prison to do some volunteer work, which had built their reputation for helping others.

One-day Shawn's wife went to the prison to do some volunteer work, and she met a man that she connected with spiritually. He was old and weary looking. It was the guard that rapped Yolanda. As they began to talk, he unraveled his criminal past to her, stating that God was with him even in all the dirt he did to others. Shawn's wife just told him to be strong and pray. The security guard was getting too old to work, and wanted to retire, if he didn't die from AIDS complications first. The Prison staff never knew that he rapped so many inmates and visitors over the years because nobody ever came forth to tell their story. They thought he was just getting old and sickly looking.

After having a few discussions with the old prison guard, Shawn's wife was curious about her husband's past. She found out that the old man she connected with spiritually was Isaiah's dad, Shawn's biological father. She was shocked but glad that in a way she'd found someone in Shawn's family who could possibly shed some light about his father since his mother disappeared after he moved away from her. The things she'd found out was for her own self-gratification, and to pass along to her children, because she loved him no matter what.

Shawn had become so successful, that his past was just a memory. His wife was no longer a teacher, and she had become a full-time volunteer at the Prison, and home-schooled their children while they were small. Money was never an issue with Shawn's family. He lavished his wife with gifts and all the finer things in life. He knew she truly appreciated him for who he was and not for what he could give her. His children grew up, and attended the best private schools the west coast had to offer. They'd turned past greed into greatness! They loved and lived the best life they could....Together.

Maria's mom and sister, Basila, and Adora were the beneficiaries of her estate. They stayed in the glass house that Michael had built for him and Patricia, but they took care of everything that Maria inherited. After all, she deserved it with all that she endured. In memory of Maria, they'd kept the home decorated the way that Maria had left it.

After Shawn revealed most of his past to his wife, they'd met Maria's family through community service. They all shared stories of what happened in the past, and even unselfishly shared some of their inheritance. Even though time had passed, Shawn was still hurt by the abandonment of his father, and abuse by his mother LaShawn. He'd remembered she inflicted much pain upon him as a child. He visited his father Isaiah's final resting place each time with much regret and wondering what his life was really like.

FOR LOVE OR MONEY?

LaShawn just disappeared from the face of the earth. She had lost her son and Isaiah because of the abuse and hatred. Her old boyfriend Fred was still living in his ghetto world all thugged out, and he eventually found someone *more fitted* to date him.

The security guard had gotten old, still sick, yet still making it hard for new inmates. Once Shawn found out the security guard was his grandfather, he went to visit him in the prison. Nothing positive came of it; Shawn just needed a peace of mind, and to know a little bit about where he came from.

Renee and Laura hated their sister Patricia's lifestyle, and hoped she was better off where ever she was. Renee had divorced her "invisible" husband; he was never there for her. Perhaps that's why she was always in someone else's business. And "perfect" lil Laura and her husband remained close in their marriage and continued praying together.

Kenny remained in Prison for the greed and murder of Maria. The deadly HIV was taking his life slowly. It was a shame that he had nothing left and no one visited him, so suffering alone was enough, besides losing his freedom for seventy-five years for murder.

Jason and Ronald had become friends before he'd passed away. Jason found who he really was, regretted the night he'd met Yolanda, and went back to his wife, and never cheated again.

After Dr. Patricia Brown lost her medical License and practice, Regina and Sarah found jobs in another Doctor's office. But they were always skeptical about who they worked for. And, Regina cleaned up her appearance. Because no one would hire her looking like a hooker.

Even though Janice won her case against Dr. Patricia, she had nothing to get. Dr. Patricia was broke after her divorce; over the years, she'd spent most of her money on Yolanda. Janice visited Michael's gravesite from time to time. He was the one who gave her back her dignity. Sadly, she was always paranoid about Doctor's visits now.

But her husband stuck by her through all of her trials and tribulations and supported her every step of the way.

Unfortunately, no one ever visited Yolanda, or Patricia's gravesite. They were not even missed because of all the greed, lust, abuse and betrayal that they imposed on others. They were soon forgotten because of their selfish and infatuated love for money.

However, it wasn't the money that caused Patricia's, Yolanda's, or Kenny's life, career, and *friendships* to dwindle; it was the greed of it.

THE END

A Special "Thank You" to "FOR LOVE OR MONEY?" First Fans!

Mzjubilee
Stephanie C.
Martin P.
Matrina W.
Vernica D.
G.W Lawrence
June B.
Cecily P.
Eric D.
Chanda C.
James D.
Chelle
Allen J.
Valerie H.
Cheryl D.
Sonya S.
Rosemary J.
Larry O.J
Keith P.
Ingrid P.
Cheryl C.
Telecia P.
Cassie P.
Beverly H.
Patsy W.
M.V Lady
Janise S.
Author Bonnie (Puddyn)
Joyce T.
Eboni E.
Author Marcus J.
Melvin E. (Keep it real)
Veronica P.
Andrea W.
Martha T.

Deandra L.
Roslyn (Roz)
Brown Suga
Latonya M.
Derrick C.
Lisa J.
Marsha
Jill J.
Gavin P.
Ronay
Brenda P.
Ryan B.
Winora H.
Terry S.
Cathy S.
Morgan M.
Shelby C.
MV Lady
Laketa K.
J. Panders
Tawanna W.
Jonathan